HOT DADDY PACKAGE

A HOT SINGLE DAD ROMANCE #5

ANGEL DEVLIN

TRACY LORRAINE

A NOTE

Hot Daddy Package is written in British English and contains British spelling and grammar. This may appear incorrect to some readers when compared to US English books.

Angel & Tracy xo

CHAPTER ONE

Scott

Rolling over as smoothly and as silently as I can, I swing my legs from the bed and prepare to leave. I don't do the whole sleepover thing. That only gives women the impression that there might be more here than the terms they agreed to when they allowed me into their bed.

I have two rules. One, always wrap the beast. Two, never allow a woman to believe there could be a second round.

I love women. I love their eyes, their curves, their tight, pink pussies and the little noises they make when I have my fingers, or rather my cock, buried deep inside them. But as much as I might love them, I have no intention of one being a permanent fixture in my life. When you have someone permanent, they can leave. It could be by choice, or not, but somehow, they will always leave. It's a fact.

So I make sure I never get attached and more importantly, they don't get attached. It might sound like a sad way to live, but I love my life. Five nights out of seven I can safely say I'll be testing out someone else's bed, or sofa, or wall for that matter. I've got great friends who never question my choices. I have a job I love, a boss I love to piss off, and a colleague I love to wind up to the point I think she might claw my eyes out with her bottle opener.

Picking up the used condom I abandoned on the floor a few moments ago, I drop it into the bin and make quick work of pulling my clothes on. I don't need to worry about making too much noise because the woman I picked up tonight is snoring like a fucking freight train. A smile tugs at my lips; at least she enjoyed herself.

I close her front door and pull up the Uber app on my phone. I only live a couple of miles away but like fuck am I walking there in the pissing down rain at two am.

By the time I get down from the sixth floor of her building, the Uber is sitting outside waiting for me.

I jump in the back and get settled.

"Good night?" The driver asks looking at me in the interior mirror. I didn't bother checking my appearance before escaping her flat so I can only imagine that I look like I've been fucked six ways from Sunday. I should fucking hope so after she pulled at my hair like it was the thing that was sending her to heaven. That of course was my cock which she tended to with a little more of a gentle touch.

"Yeah, man. Great night."

He chuckles as he turns back to the road and pulls away from the curb. His name is familiar, but I probably spend as much time in the back of an Uber as I do my flat so there's a very good chance that this isn't my first journey with this guy.

We're outside my building in minutes and I'm heading towards my shower and then bed.

Okay, so I have a third rule. Never go to bed smelling like women whose world I rocked. Chances are I'll be running late for work tomorrow and like fuck do I want to have the stench of their perfume in my nose all day. It's bad enough that Suki smells like a fucking florist. It's about the only thing that's feminine about the bartender I love to hate.

Everyone thinks it's because I want to fuck her. I can understand why they'd think that, she's female after all, but little do they know, I have got some fucking standards and Suki fucking Madden doesn't hit them.

She's attractive. Sure. She's got a banging little body. Yes, I'll admit that. But, man, is she a raging fucking bitch.

Pushing open my front door, I begin stripping my clothes from my body and dropping them wherever they fall as I make my way to the bathroom. Turning the shower on, I step under it before it has chance to warm up. I shiver, but I don't have time to hang around. I need sleep before my early shift at the restaurant tomorrow.

I'm a waiter. The best fucking waiter InHale has ever seen I'll have you know, and there's no fucking chance I'll risk my job there. I'm onto a good thing. The owner is a legend and he pays damn well, plus his food is da shit and I get to eat it whenever the fuck I like; just like pussy come to think of it.

Once I'm confident I've replaced that chick's perfume with my own bodywash, I rub a towel over my hair and my body before diving face first into bed forgoing the effort of pulling any clothes on. I'd rather let it all hang out anyway. Not like anyone's going to see it.

SURE AS SHIT, when my alarm eventually stirs me to life and I force my eyes open, I'm late.

"Bollocks."

Dragging my body to the wardrobe, I pull on my work uniform, book my Uber, brush my teeth, and run some wax through my hair, thankful for my shower after sex rule when the scent of my bodywash hits me.

With a quick nod at myself in the mirror, I head out.

The cold hits me the second I pull the building's front door open. My breath comes out in clouds as I cross my arms over my chest wondering why I didn't have the brain power to grab a coat.

I blame the lingering alcohol from last night and race towards the car waiting for me.

Resting my head back on the head rest, I close my eyes and wish that I was still in bed with a good few hours of sleep ahead of me, but instead I'm closing in on the fancy side of town ready to stare into the delightfully evil eyes of my co-worker. Our boss, Jenson, knows we spend most of our time trying to piss each other off as much as possible, so it always amazes me when I look at the shift rota to find us on the same shifts.

As the car comes to a stop on the pavement outside the restaurant, I spot her through the glass. A little excitement sizzles in my belly. I love watching her get fired up. Her eyes alight with passion, her lips curl, and her chest heaves as she tries to work out her retaliation. I'm not embarrassed to admit that my main aim every shift is to see that look on her. It's almost become an obsession.

She's busy arranging bottles behind the bar when I walk in. She doesn't notice my arrival. I walk right up to her so she has no choice but to crash into me when she stands.

Leaning forward, I whisper in her ear. "Mornin', Kitten."

Her gasp of fear makes it all worth it. That's soon forgotten though when she stands faster than I was anticipating and slams the back of her head into my nose.

I assume it's an accident. That's until she turns her cold eyes on me and I find amusement there, alongside a smirk of her bright-red lips.

"Oops," she says, covering her mouth with her hand, doing a fucking shit impression of trying to look innocent. Suki is anything but fucking innocent. I'd put everything I own on it. She's a little wildcat. I bet she fucking scratches too.

My eyes stream with water, but thankfully when I wipe at my nose, there's no blood.

"If you'd gone to bed a little earlier last night, you might be a little more alert this morning." Her hand lands on her hip as she juts it out, her bad attitude rolling off her.

My teeth grind and my jaw pops as I stare at her. She's wearing a little red dress that I'm sure would be obscene on most women but seeing as Suki is about as tall as most ten-year-olds it sits mid-thigh. She's got sky-high red heels on as usual, but they still only bring the top of her head to my chest, forcing her to look up at me when I step forward.

"Jealous? We both know you were in bed alone in your fluffy pyjamas with a sappy fucking romance novel before eight pm last night."

"I might have been in my own bed, unlike you, but I can assure you there was no romance novel. More... researching where I can hide a body and not be caught."

"Oh I did plenty of *body* research last night."

"You're such a mutt. Go and wash the girl from your neck and get the fuck to work." My hand instinctively lifts to my neck and her laugh makes me want to wrap it tightly around hers instead.

Our stare holds, hate crackling between us. I open my mouth to shoot an insult back but sadly, we're interrupted.

"Can you two rip shreds from each other when we've not got a breakfast queue forming outside," Jenson calls, stepping into the restaurant with us.

"You got it, boss. I'm all ready to go," Suki sings sweetly, smiling at our boss like butter wouldn't fucking melt.

"Suck up," I whisper and just about move fast enough so the heel of her shoe doesn't connect with my shin.

By the time I get to the welcome stand, the queue is stretching well down the street. It's been this way since Jenson's first appearance in The Sunday Times. This place was busy before but fuck, it's insane now. I'd love to know what that smug bastard's making out of this place.

When I look back, Suki is busying herself with the coffee machine, doing anything to avoid looking at me, and a couple of other waiters appear from out of the back ready to get this shit started. I give them a nod, then open the doors.

The morning flies and my banter with the customers, or more my flirting with the females, ensures I'm constantly entertained and maintain the devil stares from Suki from her hiding place behind the polished bar.

I love our customers. Getting to talk to such a wide range of interesting people is just one of the things that keeps me here, but knowing I have Suki's attention every time I so much as look at a female is what really keeps my flirting at a level that even makes me cringe at times. I can't help it, my need to piss her off knows no bounds. If it weren't for the way she looks at me like she wants to carve up my dick with her lemon knife, then I might think she was jealous.

We're well into our lunch service when a group of four women descend and are seated in my area.

I'm too far away from the bar to physically hear it but Suki's groan rings out loud and clear in my mind. I glance over at her and find her glaring back at me, her eyes rolling so much I might be worried they might fall out if I cared.

My lip curls up into my trademark panty-melting smile and she mimics shooting herself in the temple before turning away to fulfil an order.

With my smile still in place, I head over to my new diners. "Good afternoon. What brings you beautiful ladies here today?"

Every single one of them melts when they glance up at me. Two of them actually do a double take, which does awesome things for my already over-inflated ego.

"It's Jenna's thirtieth," one of them says, batting her eyelashes at me. "We're planning on knocking a few things off her bucket list."

Glancing over at her friend, a bright red blush covers her cheeks. My excitement level immediately kicks up a notch. Leaning forward, I make eye contact with each before focusing back on the birthday girl.

"That sounds intriguing. Tell me more." Birthday Girl opens and closes her mouth a few times like a fucking fish, but no words leave her lips. Instead, when I hear a voice, it's really not the one I'm expecting.

"Scott," a shrill Suki screeches across the busy restaurant. It's like nails on a chalkboard and immediately makes my spine stiffen.

"My apologies, ladies. It seems I'm required elsewhere. I'll be right back." I give them a wink before standing to full height and turning.

My eyes almost pop out of my head when they land on Suki and what's in her arms.

CHAPTER TWO

Suki

Staring at myself in the bathroom mirror, I wonder if I'm up to a day of dealing with Scott Sullivan. I'd had a disturbed night's sleep with dreams about my family, or lack thereof. I'll have to give Carl a ring, I think, and see if he wants to come over for tea one night this week. I wonder what I'll do when he eventually meets a girl and settles down. Because the fact my cousin is single is, I'm sure, one of the main reasons why the offer of a hot home-cooked meal has him agree to come around to my flat and put up with my scintillating conversation once or twice a week.

I had a sex dream about Scott. The thought makes my lips pull into a grimace and has me stepping quickly into the shower like I need to wash the dream off. Ugh. Don't get me wrong, the guy looks like a walking sex god, but his personality... he's... oily, smarmy, smug, conceited, a dickhead. I'd go on, but I don't have all day. I find the constant banter between us exhausting, yet it makes my shift go quicker. There's a love/hate thing about when we're on shift at the same time, which is more frequently than not, despite my boss' wife, Leah, telling me she'd asked Jenson to put us on opposite shifts when I first started there and the animosity between us had become apparent.

He just doesn't seem to have a personality. Women are so fucking shallow. All they see is the outside of him and they're smitten, and then he turns on the charm and they're like lost rats following the Pied Piper. Only here the Pied Piper is a King Rat. *Fucking hell, Suki, you've spent half of your shower thinking about Scott.* I get annoyed with myself and scrub myself down harder than absolutely necessary. I finish getting ready and get to work.

On a morning shift, I'm mainly working the coffee machine as the breakfast and brunch rush begins, although some people start their day with Mimosas or straight champagne. I could do with being drunk myself today. I'm tired and have already had to put up with Scott's crap. We're now starting the lunch rush and he's taken about eight phone numbers already today.

"Everything okay, Suki?" Jenson asks, his head slightly tilted as he looks at me. I straighten up. "Yes, boss. I'm just feeling a bit tired today. Hope I'm not sickening for something."

"Me too. I need my best bartender here." He looks at me closer. "If you need to take five though at any time, or go home, just let me know, and I'll get someone to cover for you."

"I'll be okay, I'm sure. Scott seems to have the customers handled. They don't seem all that interested in drinks." I nod over to where he's taking orders and schmoozing. He runs a hand through his shaggy hair and pouts. I groan. "Why they fall for that I don't know."

"Well, it helps business, so I don't mind at all." Jenson grins.

"How come I'm almost always on shift with him when you know we hate each other?" I ask. Then I want to fling my hand over my mouth. It's the question I've always pondered but never let loose.

"Suki. Have you not read reviews of the restaurant at all?" Jenson's mouth has a quirk to it.

"No."

"So you've not seen TripAdvisor?"

"That's for holidays, isn't it?"

He shakes his head. "Not anymore. Now it also has reviews for restaurants. You should take a look and then you'll see why you and Scott are put on shifts together a lot. It's not just good food and The Sunday Times reviews that brings people to InHale regularly."

With that he wanders through to his office, and I make a mental note to look at TripAdvisor later to see what he's talking about.

Right now though I can see a woman walking towards me with a baby in her arms. "What can I get you?" I ask, noting the sweat on her upper lip and her wide eyes. She looks around and her eyes alight on Scott who's just come out of the kitchen.

She moves the baby in her arms until it's passed across the bar. I automatically take hold of it, waiting for her to say she has cramp or something. "Tell Scott it's his." She says and she walks off.

"Hey. Hey there, lady. What are you doing? Come back." I shout, but the woman is wearing trainers to my high heels and I have a baby in my arms and she does not. She runs out of the restaurant and doesn't look back.

I look down at the baby in shock. It only looks a few weeks old. What the fuck just happened? She can't just give me a baby and run off. We need to call the police. But she said it's Scott's. The sly dog. He kept that one quiet, that one of his swimmers escaped. The baby is fast asleep. It has a white sleepsuit on and the finest smattering of dark hair. I can't tell if it's a boy or a girl, but as an awful smell hits my nostrils, I do know that it needs a nappy change. My final lot of foster parents used to take in babies and left me to look after them ninety percent of the time, so I know my way around a baby, and the fact the woman dropped it off without so much as a changing bag makes alarm bells ring even more.

I watch as Scott flirts with a table of four women for a little too long. He's not rushing to take the order into the kitchen and I can't handle this smell any longer so I scream over to him, "Scott."

I can see the annoyance on his features as he excuses himself from the group of horny, enthralled women and he heads towards me and then his eyes widen and he gasps. "What the fuck is that smell and why do you have a baby in your arms. Whose is it?"

"Yours apparently."

It's a good job I didn't hand him the baby because he'd have dropped it.

"You're hilarious, Suki. Were you jealous I was giving those women all of my attention? Now seriously, go change its stinking nappy or give it back to mummy because I'm going to be sick."

Oh dear. He's not getting it. I stand staring at him waiting for him to understand.

"What the fuck is wrong with you? Stop staring at me. We don't do this. You give me shit. I give you shit. That's how this goes. You don't stand there silently staring."

I hold out the baby. "That is what I'm doing. I'm giving you shit. It's in your baby's nappy. Now take it. I don't see why I should have my arms falling off holding it and have to smell that."

"Suki, I'm starting to worry for your mental health. That. Is. Not. My. Baby."

"Scott." I talk to him slowly so he can begin to understand. "A woman just came in. She handed me this baby. Said to give it to you and then she ran out of the restaurant."

He doesn't look as haughty anymore. Now he's looking at me like I'm stupid which really gets my back up.

"A woman gave you a baby and ran out of the restaurant and you didn't call the police or anything?"

"No because she said it was yours. I'm not going to call the police and say 'oh, officer, a mum has run off and left her baby with its father'. That's most mothers at six pm in an evening, mate."

I hold the baby out now in a way that he has to get hold of it. "Here you go, Daddy."

"It's not my baby, Suki. I don't know whose it is, but we need to do something."

I put my hands on my hips. "*We* don't need to do something. *You* need to do something. Starting with changing its nappy."

Panic begins to soak through Scott's features and he looks at the bundle in his hands. The smell isn't getting any better though the baby has now opened its eyes.

"Aww, you're a cutie, apart from your smelly bum." I tell it.

"What do I do?"

Scott's desperation in his question has me on alert. Mr Cool, Calm, and Collected is becoming ruffled.

"I don't know how to change a nappy and I don't know what to do about this baby. How do I know it's mine and how do I deal with its mother having dumped it if it is?"

Then I see a calmness settle on him as he exhales. "Oh God, I get it now."

"You do?"

"Mummy's gone to buy some nappies. She obviously forgot the changing bag, passed the baby to you and she'll be back soon. She'll have not said to give the baby to me at all. She'll have said give my love to Scott or something."

"Now you're the one with mental problems. You're delusional, because that's not what she said."

He flinches at my words, then recovers himself, but now his voice is like steel. "Oh look, Jenson's there."

We walk towards our boss.

"Whose baby is it? I've been watching you two and it's cute, but you need to be working, we're busy."

I say it's Scott's at the same time Scott says it's a customer's.

"My office, now." Jenson demands.

Once we're inside and sat on the two seats opposite his desk, Jenson leans forward. "Suki, explain why you think this is Scott's baby."

I go through the last half an hour of my shift.

Jenson begins to look concerned. "I'll look at the CCTV footage and then Scott, you can tell us if you know the woman."

"I'm not being funny, Jenson, but he's shagged that many women it probably won't ring a bell." I add.

"It's a start. Suki, would you mind popping to the supermarket and getting some things for cleaning this baby up. I'll write you a list and give you some money."

"I know what to get. I looked after babies a lot when I was younger." I stand up and Jenson goes in the drawer to get me some money. I hold my hand up. "It's fine. I'll put it on my credit card and

Scott can pay me back when the bill comes in if the baby's his."

The baby starts wailing. "The sooner we get that nappy changed the better. I'll be back." I leave and head towards the supermarket.

I buy the items the baby might need if mum doesn't reappear anytime soon. I actually quite enjoy adding the cute little sleeveless vests, bibs, and other paraphernalia. I get colic treatment, Sudocrem and baby wipes, along with nappies, a changing mat, and some bath stuff. I add a couple of ready-made milk drinks to my pile and smart a little at the total at the checkout. My arms drag as I carry everything back.

"Trust a woman to get carried away shopping," Scott says like the true dick he is. Even Jenson looks at him exasperated.

"Scott, that's a fraction of what you'll need if this baby is yours. You need to thank Suki for going and getting all this for you."

That shuts him up.

"Right, Suki, are you okay changing and cleaning the baby up while I get up the CCTV or do you want me to do it as I'm more than used to it?" Jenson asks.

"I'll do it and Scott can help. He'll need to know what to do."

Scott pfffts. "It's not mine and so I don't need to be involved. At all."

Ignoring him, I set up everything on Jenson's desk. Then I take the baby out of his arms and place it on the table.

"I'm going to take my laptop over to the bar outside." Jenson declares, leaving us to it.

I strip baby out of its clothing, wipes and nappies etc at the ready, and then I pull off the nappy.

Scott takes one look at the baby poop and as the smell hits his nostrils he heaves, actual full on gips as he holds his nose.

I look at the baby's bottom area.

"Congrats, Daddy." I tell him. "It's a girl."

CHAPTER THREE

Scott

This is a joke, right? It's Suki's idea to get me to freak the fuck out about all the women I've slept with. Well, let me tell you right this fucking second that this shit isn't funny. And the smell coming from this baby's rear end is even less amusing. There's no way I could have had a hand in making something that smells so fucking bad.

My stomach turns when I get a look at the mess that's making the smell.

Wait a minute... is that chicken fucking korma?

I lean in a little to make sure the baby is real, and this isn't a practical joke gone very, very wrong but nope, just like I feared, that is one real life living baby.

Suki says something but with the amount of blood rushing past my ears, I don't hear a single word of it.

My eyes zero in on what's she's doing. She makes quick work of wiping the baby clean before pulling the rotten nappy away and replacing it with a clean one. The amount of poppers on the front of the thing it's wearing damn near blows my mind, but Suki makes it look easy as she does it up before tickling the babies tummy, making it coo with delight.

Something happens when the noise hits my ears. My heart clenches like I never felt before, making breathing a fucking challenge.

"Are you okay?" Suki asks, looking genuinely concerned for the first time since I met her. It's not an expression I'm all that overly keen on seeing. I much prefer her 'what the fuck?' face.

"I..." I stare at the baby before me now wiggling about on top of Jenson's desk. I *really* look for the first time since Suki handed it over. I stare into a pair of dark brown eyes and it feels like I'm looking in a mirror.

Realisation hits like a fucking articulated lorry. *This kid is fucking mine.*

My heart races, my chest heaves, but I'm not able to drag in the air I need and the room spins around me.

I vaguely hear Suki's voice again but nothing registers, only her light touch on my arm as she guides me back down onto the chair I was previously sitting on before getting a very quick and smelly lesson in nappy changing.

Fuck. What the actual fuck?

"I... I can't do this. I can't look after a baby. I can barely look after myself."

"Good to know we agree on something." The sarcasm in Suki's voice is what has me looking up, but when I find her face, she's anything but amused.

"Suki, I can't... I..." *Fuck.* Slumping down in the chair, I drop my head into my hands. I hear movement when the baby starts complaining but I don't look up. I'm too lost in my own panic. I can't look after a baby. I don't have the slightest idea how to even start.

"Scott," her voice sounds alien to the one I'm

used to, and it has me lifting my head. "I know you're scared. I know this is huge, but your daughter needs you to try to hold it together right now."

My daughter. My daughter?

"It's a girl?"

Suki rolls her eyes and my frustration grows. "You did just watch me change her nappy right? Where I said it's a girl?"

"I guess I wasn't paying attention."

"Well, you'd better start paying attention, Daddy."

"Don't call me that."

"Why? This little girl here is most definitely yours. You've looked at her right?"

"I have," I admit. I'm not sure I like the fact the similarities between us are that noticeable.

The door opens and Jenson reappears. "Suki, get that stinky nappy out of here."

She hesitantly hands the baby over and once she's happy that I've got her securely in my arms, she picks up the bag full of shit and leaves us to it.

"Here." Jenson places his laptop down on the desk in front of me and hits play from a little earlier this morning.

I stare at the slightly fuzzy footage as a woman

holding a baby walks in. I've no idea if I'm horrified or relieved that I recognise her instantly. Suki would normally be right about not recognising my conquests but there was something about this one, probably the fact that I fucked her in a dark back alley after spending all night dancing with her. It was her birthday. I remember telling her that I'd give her an extra special present. Turns out I gave her more than either of us was bargaining for. I might be adventurous when it comes to sex but that was my first time in an alley and I like to remember my firsts at least. Doesn't mean I remember her name though, if she even gave it to me.

"Jesus," I mutter, looking down to the little wriggling bundle in my arms.

"You recognise her?"

"Yep, I fu—" I cut myself off when I remember that I am actually talking to my boss right now. "I had a *moment* with her about..."

"Eleven months ago?" he asks, his smirk firmly in place.

"About that, yeah. Fuck."

"Everything's going to be fine. This might be the best thing that's ever happened to you," he says, his eyes softening, probably as he thinks about his own kids. "I did it on my own for years, I've no doubt that you're more than capable."

"I'm not so sure I share your confidence." And as if she's agreeing, the baby starts wailing in my arms.

"She probably needs feeding."

"I'll grab something from the kitchen in a minute."

He laughs and my brows draw together. "She needs milk, Scott. Suki bought some." He rummages around in the bags she dropped to the floor not so long ago and pulls out a carton and a bottle. "I'll go and sterilise it and warm it for her. You sit tight." And then he's gone, leaving me alone for the first time ever with a baby. My baby.

Her cries continue and I sit staring at her not having a single fucking clue how to make this any better. I was going to feed the kid some dauphinoise potatoes or whatever I could find in the kitchen. I am so not equipped to be responsible for such a small person.

Her cries get louder, her little face turning beetroot red. Fuck knows how she's gone from quiet and contented to wanting to blow the fucking roof off the place in about thirty seconds flat but hey ho. I guess I do get a little hangry at times too.

"Shhh," I soothe, but it does very little, I swear all she does is frown at me. "It's okay, Jenson will be back with food soon." Still she cries and I sigh. "I should probably apologise before this day gets any crazier. I'm sorry you're stuck with me as a daddy. But I promise to try my best. What good that might do I'm not sure, but just give me a break, yeah?"

Silence surrounds us as she blinks up at me. I swear I see a smile or something twitch at the corner of her lips. My chest constricts as we continue staring at each other. It's like we already know each other yet can't believe we're actually together. It's a weird as fuck feeling and totally unsettling.

"See, all she needed was to hear your voice until it was ready," Jenson says walking into the room.

"You were listening?" I'm not sure if I'm embarrassed or just downright mortified.

"It was sweet. I always knew you had a softer side. This should be a walk in the park for you; you sweet talk women every minute of the day." He winks and I groan.

"I'm not sure this is the same thing."

"No, maybe not. This one will still be next to you in the morning."

The thought of taking her home terrifies me.

"Hold out your wrist." I look up at Jenson, confused as fuck as he squirts a little of the milk onto my exposed wrist when I do as I'm told. "You feel how warm that is?"

"Uh... I guess."

"That's what it should be like." I nod, completely bewildered by all of this. He places the bottle in my hand, and I move it towards her mouth. Her lips part immediately and she sucks the teat into her mouth.

"Wow, she's got some power." I don't mean it to sound suggestive but when Jenson barks out a laugh, I realise exactly how it sounded. "Shit, I didn't... fuck."

"You're a natural. She's so relaxed with you."

"I'm glad one of us is."

"You'll soon get used to it. It's a tough learning curve being a parent but we all just figure it out as we go."

"At least you had nine months to get used to the idea. I didn't even get nine minutes."

"True. I've got every confidence in you." I appreciate his sentiment, but I can't say I'm feeling even an ounce of his optimism. "Give her a break and lift her over your shoulder. You need to gently tap her back until she burps."

"Burps?"

"Yeah. Drinking that fast will give her wind. You need to help her bring it up."

"Right." I somehow manage to manoeuvre her without dropping her onto the floor beneath her and after only thirty seconds of tapping her back, she lets out the most impressive burp. "So maybe she is mine," I say with a laugh.

I return to feeding her and Jenson watching, I feel his stare burning into me despite the fact I don't take my eyes away from my daughter. *My daughter...* there are two words I never thought I'd say.

"Okay, I'm giving you the week off. I'd love to give you more but at such short notice it might be an issue. I'll do everything I can. I suggest you get out of here and try to get sorted."

"What am I meant to do? Just take her home and what? Let her sleep in the bottom drawer?"

"No, I wouldn't do that. Go to your aunts, take a bit of time to get your head together. I'll phone Leah and we'll make sure you've got everything you need. Call us when you're headed home and we'll meet you there."

"I can't ask you to—"

"You didn't. I'm offering. Now get the hell out of here. I've got a restaurant to run, not a creche.

With a sleeping baby in one arm and the bags Suki appeared with in the other, I make my way out of Jenson's office. It's the most surreal moment of my life. I arrived at work this morning like it was a normal day and I'm leaving... a father. This is some seriously fucked up shit.

I'm almost at the main doors when Suki spots me. She's busy shaking a cocktail and has a huddle of customers around her bar, so I don't stop to chat. Instead I give her a friendly nod, thanking for her what she's done for the little lady in my arms and step from the restaurant.

It's still freezing cold but thanks to the all-in-one polar bear looking suit Suki bought at least I don't need to worry that she's cold.

I carefully climb into the back of the Uber that's idling waiting for me and get an inquisitive look off the driver when I strap myself into the seat and hold the baby close to me.

"No car seat?"

"Wasn't planned, but I'll get it sorted for future."

He nods and pulls away. He must see all sorts doing this job. I can't imagine this is the weirdest situation he's been in.

I don't warn my aunt I'm coming. I wouldn't know what to say even if I did. *"Hey, I'm just popping around so you can meet my daughter."* I can only imagine how well that would have gone down. Not that turning up on her doorstep clutching a baby to my chest is going to be any less of a shock.

CHAPTER FOUR

Suki

I didn't want to leave the office when Jenson told me to go back to the bar. I wanted to care for the baby. For the rest of my shift I'm like an Oscar-winning movie actress because the smile on my face to customers is completely false. My brain whirrs with everything that happened. It stirs up memories of my own past. I need Carl. I send him a text and ask if I can go to his place for dinner and a drink. Fuck, it's Saturday night. I bet he has plans.

After a bewildered Scott has left with his

daughter, I ask Jenson if I can have the rest of the day off to go and help him.

"He's okay, Suki. He's on his way to his auntie's house."

"Oh."

"I can give you his mobile number if you like, so you can check how he's doing later?"

A smile finally breaks across my face. "All the times that guy has asked me if I want it and I've told him where to go. Yes please. I'm good with kids. I want to help. Did he know the mother?" ·

Jenson nodded. "He remembered her but not a name or anything, so how he's going to track her down, goodness knows. I guess he needs to call the police?"

I shrug. "The baby's probably better off without a mum like that."

"She might need help."

"She didn't look like she needed help. She was dressed to the nines and coherent. It was the baby who had nothing."

Jenson stares at me for a beat too long. "Well, it's up to Scott, I guess."

"Yeah. I can't imagine what must be going through his head right now."

"Extreme and utter panic." Jenson laughs. "I

know you don't get along, but Scott needs all the help he can get right now. So I appreciate you offering to help him. I know what being a single dad is like. It's not easy."

"Yeah and I know what being an abandoned baby is like." I confess.

His eyes widen. "Shit, Suki. I had no idea."

I shrug my shoulders. "Why would you? I don't talk about it."

"Were you abandoned like that? Left somewhere?" Jenson leans over and puts a hand on my arm. "Sorry, I'm being nosy. You don't have to answer that."

"No it's okay." I take a deep breath. "My childhood was spent in foster care or in care homes. I found out when I was eighteen that my mother was fourteen when she had me. My grandparents made her give me up and didn't want anyone to know she'd ever been pregnant and that suited her. I contacted her when I reached adulthood and she didn't want to know. Actually, she offered to pay me off. She's a trophy wife of an art critic. I'm not good for publicity."

"That's awful."

I nod. "She gave me my father's details though. My dad died in a road traffic accident at just seventeen years old. But I'm now in touch with my paternal grandparents and I have a paternal auntie and they have a son, Carl, my cousin. He's lovely, reached out to me and we're quite close now."

"Jesus, Suki. We ought to form a club 'Survivors of mothers who walked'."

"Yeah, it's not something that's really talked about is it? Everyone always thinks mothers love their children and would give their life for them, but my mother, although pressured to give me up, showed she moved on; your wife chose her career, and who knows why Scott's baby mama has done what she's done."

"Knowing how I feel about my kids, I just can't even try to understand it. The only thing I do know is that if a mother—or any parent for that matter—doesn't have enough love for their kid, then their kid is better off without them, even if you end up on a rocky road somewhere else."

"Yeah, she screwed my life up for sure, but I haven't missed out from what I've seen so far."

"Well, today has certainly been one hell of a day. If he needs you, Suki, ring me and I'll sort staffing."

"But we're so busy."

"Yeah, but you've reminded me what's important. It's not the business, it's that baby."

"Like you say, Scott might be okay with his auntie."

"She's getting on in years though, and I worry he might just consider parking his daughter there and absolving himself of his responsibilities. He needs to step up."

Jenson looks at me pointedly.

"Okay. I'll check in and I'll make sure he does what he needs to do."

"Who better to order him about than the person who continually gives him shit over his actions? Can you wear a wire and a spy cam? Oh to be a fly on the wall as Scott gets lessons in fatherhood."

We both laugh, lost in our imaginations.

"Right, I'd better get on and the bar has a queue now I've distracted you. You'd better get back to it before Leona kills me for chatting to you for so long. I need to keep her sweet in case she's needed for overtime."

I say my goodbyes and apologising to my fellow bartender, I finish out my shift.

. . .

CARL SAYS he has no plans and offers to send for a Chinese takeaway. I arrive at seven to be greeted by a huge bear hug. My cousin is amazing. He's muscly and tall and always warm and gives the kind of cuddles you need when you're fed up. I was closed off and defensive when I first met him, but Carl doesn't take much notice of anything like that. He hugged me as soon as he met me and said it was the Taylor way. I told him I was a Madden, although actually that name belongs to my first set of foster parents, so I'm not really anything but the name they gave me, Suki.

And that has me thinking of Baby Sullivan. We don't know her name.

"What's wrong? You look like someone just died. Come in. I thought you were just calling round to catch up. Why didn't you tell me something was up?"

I wave a hand in front of my face. "Nah, it's not me. Not really. It's Scott."

"Oh God, what's he done now? Are you sure I can't go and punch him for you?"

I've moaned about Scott many, many times to Carl, and when he's been to InHale I've had to beg him to leave Scott alone and not thump him.

"It's not like that. A woman came in today with a baby. She said it was his and just handed it over."

Carl's mouth drops open. "You're shitting me? Just here you go, Scott?"

"No, he was serving. She passed the kid to me. The baby's only a couple of months old. It's definitely his though. She's his spitting image."

"Yeah, I'd still be needing a DNA test. So tell me all. Tell you what. I'll call in our order and then you can update me while we wait."

So I do. I tell him how Scott is now probably at his aunties.

"But the thing is, Carl. I can't stop thinking about the baby. Because I was once that baby. Baby no name abandoned by my mum."

"Ah, now I get it. It's bringing your past up."

"Scott has no idea what he's doing and I do. I know how to look after a baby. I'm going to offer to teach him. To help."

"But you can't stand the guy."

"We're going to have to put our issues aside because until he finds the mum, that baby has to be the priority. He didn't even know how to change a nappy. I reckon he was spoiled rotten as a kid; probably treated like a complete prince and never had to lift a finger. I've totally made my mind up anyway. Tomorrow is my day off and I'm going to call him and arrange to go to his place and see what he needs to set himself up for life as a dad."

"Oh, Suki. I'm not sure you should get involved. Are you sure this is about Scott and the baby and helping or are you somehow trying to sort out your past?"

I stare at the floor. "I honestly don't know. I just saw that baby. She's absolutely gorgeous, Carl. And I just wanted her to be happy. I couldn't face knowing that Scott landed her on his auntie and went back to his ladykilling ways."

"He's just found out one of his conquests had a baby. I doubt he'll have sex ever again. Not without wrapping it in fifty condoms first."

I begin to smile. "You should have seen his face. He's such a cocky bastard in all senses of the word and he looked like he was about to shit his pants to match his daughter."

Carl sniggers. "I've got your back, Suki. You need me for anything with all this: shoulder to cry on, fixing up a cot. Just give me a shout. I'll put aside wanting to punch his lights out, for how he treats you but only because of the baby."

"You're the best cousin ever."

"I'm the only one you know you have."

"Yeah, well, I found the perfect one and don't need another."

The doorbell chimed and Carl went and got our Chinese while I sent a text to Scott.

Suki: It's Suki. Jenson gave me your number. How are things going?

I've eaten a large portion of my food before I get a ping on my phone.

Scott: My phone is now covered in shit. That's how it's going.

Suki: Oops. Have you got used to the idea of being a dad yet?

There's another pause.

Scott: Okay. I've washed my hands and my phone and now my auntie has Doe. Of course I'm used to the idea of being a dad. It's been like six fucking hours. I've even booked a nursery place. What do you think????

Suki: I'm just trying to show some concern, fuckhead. Her name is Doe???

Scott: Sorry. I'm VERY stressed right now. My auntie says I need a DNA test as soon as possible so I'll go to the docs Monday and sort that. I don't know whether to call the police as I'm scared if they see me with Doe they'll take her into care. I called her Doe because I don't know her name and I don't want to give her a proper name and then her mum comes back and I find out she's called Arabella or something. Her eyes are doe-like, plus that's the surname they give people that lose their memories isn't it? She's a Jane Doe. So her name's Doe.

Suki: She does have doe-eyes. That's cute.

Scott: You wouldn't be saying the word cute if she'd just shit on you like she did me.

Suki: *Laughing emoticons*

Scott: Anyway, my auntie is trying (and largely failing) to get me to be baby friendly. I can now make a bottle and she sent me out for a proper sterilising unit, bottles, and milk powder. How many freaking bottles do they need? Then they just sick it up and poop it out. Then winding. Changing. Ten minutes sleep and it all starts again. Is this my life now? Sorry, I'm having a panic attack. I'll be back in a minute.

I wait and then notice Carl staring at me.

"Fuck. Sorry. I was texting Scott about the baby and kind of... forgot I was here."

"Charming. Now it's not only my dates do that, but my family too."

I scrunch my eyes up. "Am I forgiven if I give you my last spare rib?"

"Absolutely." He reaches for it. "So, what's the latest?"

"He went off to have a panic attack."

"Going well then?"

My phone beeped again.

Scott: Sorry about that. Just all got a bit much. Had to stand on the back and get a breath of air.

Suki: No worries. What did your auntie say?

Scott: That she was surprised this was my first. Then she said she'd help for a couple of days, but I needed to learn fast. I was moaning about having no experience and she laid into me saying no one had any experience with their first child and to grow a pair.

Suki: I like your auntie already. Anyway, I'm offering my services.

Scott: The last thing I need right now is sex, darlin'. You're too late. *Grinning emoticons*

Suki: Arsehole personality still detected.

I'm great with kids. Meet me tomorrow at your place and let me see what you need to become baby friendly and I'll stay as long as is needed.

Scott: Stay? As in for the day?

Suki: No, I'm going to fucking move in.

But as I type the words, I wonder. Should I actually offer to do just that?

CHAPTER FIVE

Scott

I knew my auntie wasn't going to take the little bundle out of my arms and tell me she'd sort everything, but I wasn't quite expecting the reality check she gave me. I've never hidden my... lifestyle, shall we say, so my auntie is just as aware of my nightly activities as everyone else in my life. She knew, and had warned me time and time again, that this was inevitable. Those are not really the words I need right now.

"You'll be fine, Scott. Despite what you believe, you are more than capable of looking after another human being, no matter how small she may be." My auntie waves us off, and Doe and I head home with an Uber full of stuff I'm not all that confident about. Doe now has a car seat. My auntie dropped it into the car like it was the simplest of tasks. Fuck only knows how I'm meant to get the thing out again, and then her out of it once we're up in the flat.

"I hope you're prepared for what comes next, kid. It could get ugly."

It's in that moment I'm reminded of the unexpected texts from Suki not so long ago. *Did she offer to...*

My brows drag together as I dig my phone from my pocket. I scroll through the conversation that happened no less than an hour ago and reread. I wasn't in the right frame of mind when I first read the words. Pausing mid-conversation to have a mild panic attack about the situation I've found myself in sure didn't help things. But at the end of our conversation, plain and simple in black and white are her words:

Meet me tomorrow at your place and let me see what you need to become baby

friendly and I'll stay as long as is needed.

Suki's offering to come and help. Why?

My hackles rise instantly. She hates me. She probably thinks this whole situation is fucking hilarious and no less than I deserve. Is she intending to come and tell me what a shit job I'm doing already? To laugh at my complete lack of paternal skills?

Anger swirls in my stomach. There's no way she's just offering to help. She isn't that... nice.

The Uber slows to a stop as my building reveals itself and reality once again slams into my chest. My hand lifts in the hope pressing it against my heart will actually fucking help. It does fuck all. My lungs burn as I try to drag in the air I need.

I don't know if I can do this.

My hands tremble as I stare out of the window, thinking about my third-floor flat and how I'm meant to manoeuvre a baby up and down regularly.

"Are you alright, mate? Do you need a hand?"

I look to the eyes of the driver in the rear-view

mirror. It's as if I'm looking into the eyes of my fairy fucking godmother.

"Do you mind? I've kind of got a lot of stuff."

"Sure thing, man.

With the driver's help, we have everything up to my flat in under ten minutes.

I lower a still sleeping Doe to the floor and look around.

There's shit everywhere. Takeout cartons and beer cans litter my small kitchen and the coffee table. I don't even remember when the last time I ate here was, so Christ knows how long they've actually been there. There are clothes strewn about the floor, mostly in the direction of the bathroom and... what's that smell? Why didn't I notice that this morning?

Leaving Doe where she is, I throw open a couple of windows and start making the place look at least a little acceptable. I'd hate for her to open her eyes and be even more disappointed in me than she probably already is.

The kitchen surfaces are clear now the bin has been filled and emptied. It smells fresh too. I'm just unpacking the steriliser and bottle prep machine when I hear a small cry from the living room. My heart constricts, my stomach tumbles, and I run full pelt to make sure she's okay.

"Hey there, baby girl. Did you have a good sleep?" My voice comes out all soft and cooey; the exact way I hate when I hear other guys talk to their kids. I guess there really is a button inside us that makes it happen unintentionally when our baby is in front of us. I unclip her from her seat.

Shrugging at my thoughts, I slip my hands under her little arms and lift her from her seat. Her legs kick with the freedom and I bring her to my chest.

"So, this is home for now, little lady. I've tried to make it suitable for guests, but it's probably best you know from the get-go that I'm a bit of a slob." She stares at me as if she's taking in every single word before she graces me with a tiny smile that damn near melts my heart.

"Okay, so... what now, huh? You wanna eat? Poop? Watch some football?" I realise that she doesn't actually care.

She's probably just glad someone's looking after her, you dickhead, I tell myself. Thoughts of how we ended up here run through my head; total disbelief that any mother could drop their baby and run like she did.

"Oh, I know." I lay her down on the floor, noticing that I urgently need to run the vacuum around before running for the bags by the front door. "I bought you a play mat. It's got loads of colourful animals on it. You'll love it."

I shake it out beside her and then lift her onto it, gently placing her under the bar where assorted soft toys, mirrors and other bits hang down. She sucks at her little fist and it looks so endearing.

I'm pretty sure it's the first night of my adult life where I don't send my guest home once I'm bored with them, and I'm not just saying that because I literally can't send her anywhere else, but I actually never get bored of her. The different faces she makes, the cute little sounds that pass her lips. I am utterly and totally in love with this little woman and that is something I never thought I'd say in a million years. My aunt banged on about my need for a DNA test, and I do agree it needs to be done, but I already know categorically that this little girl is mine. I feel it. The connection between us already is just too strong for her not to be a part of me. No fucking way.

AS IN LOVE as I might be, our first night together is anything but smooth. I feed her, change her, do all the things exactly as my auntie instructed, but right as I lie her in the Moses basket for the night, her face turns purple and a horribly familiar smell permeates the room.

I look to my left and right, but it only confirms my fears. I'm alone and this smell is no one's to deal with but mine.

I lay the changing mat out on my bed and hope and pray that both of us, and the bed, don't end up covered in shit. My last attempt was amateur at best so I was ever hopeful that second time would be lucky, well... not lucky, I had a nappy full of shit on my hands, but... better, maybe?

Thankfully, all the crap stays in the nappy and is almost professionally deposited into the nappy bag and then into the bin in the record time of... twenty-four minutes.

With her all bundled up in her babygrow, I settle her down once again and climb into bed. Although I'm exhausted—mostly emotionally after what this day has thrown at me—I lie there with my eyes open staring at the ceiling and listening to her heavy breathing. Anytime the rhythm of it changes, I'm up and checking on her. She's fine every single time while my heart races like a motherfucker thinking that I've done something wrong.

And when she needs something? Man, do I know about it. I've just drifted off when she lets me know, none too subtly, that she needs feeding. The sleep fog had just hit me and those first few seconds, I have no fucking clue where I am or what's happening. But with her in my arms to settle her, we make our way to the kitchen and I prep her bottle thanks to the fan-fucking-tastic machine my auntie told me I had to buy. I don't need to worry about the temperature, although like the sensible parent I am, I check it anyway just like Jenson showed me. We settle back into bed and I stare down at this incredible little package I received today and wonder how I've survived this long without her in my life. I thought I needed a different woman every night of the week. Turns out I just needed a single one every fucking night.

Once she's fed, I place her down in her basket and she almost instantly falls back to sleep. Thankfully, I do the exact same thing.

THE NEXT TIME I wake it's to a happy, smiling baby and the winter sun shining through the curtains.

I change her and place her down in her basket while I make myself a coffee and her milk. I'm just burping her with a pink cloth thing thrown over my shoulder, again exactly like I've been taught, when the buzzer sounds out.

I frown. No one ever visits me. I always go to them, whoever it may be. It's one of the reasons my flat is such a shithole.

With Doe still over my shoulder, I continue to gently tap her back hoping for a burp sometime soon so the rest of her bottle doesn't go cold on her and I lean down to press the button.

"Hey, it's me." The sound of Suki's voice knocks me for six.

"Oh... uh..." I don't mean to sound like I don't want her help. I'd just totally forgotten, again, that she was coming. "C- come up." I press my hand down on the button to unlock the front door and try to ignore the rolling of my stomach. Us alone in a confined space is a recipe for disaster. Maybe I should go and hide my kitchen knives.

CHAPTER SIX

Suki

Why am I here? I'm standing outside Scott Sullivan's flat with four bags of baby stuff after a trip to a popular baby store this morning. I've maxed out my credit card and the baby is nothing to do with me. Yet she's everything to do with me at the same time. He buzzes me up and before I know it, I'm being greeted by the man himself who has Doe over his shoulder.

And oh my god if that vision doesn't actually do something to my own ovaries. The usually well-groomed Scott is a dishevelled mess, his fringe falling in his face. He's wearing grey and cream checked pyjama bottoms and a cream t-shirt accessorised by Doe. Her little nappy clad bum looks so cute with his large hand against it.

Then his mouth spoils everything and reminds me why I've come here. For the baby.

"Are you actually coming in or have you arrived early for her first birthday party?"

"Ha ha." I follow him through to his flat, kicking my shoes off in the hallway and dropping my bags down in the living room he's made me follow him to.

"So I gather you've come to check she's still alive." He drawls.

I shake my head. "No, Scott. I've come to help."

He fixes me with a weird stare. "Why would you come to help me? You must be laughing yourself to the point of pissing your pants with this situation."

"It's not funny that a baby has been abandoned by her mother. Plus, you have to admit it yourself, you don't have the first clue right now about looking after a baby. Neither can you sort out everything she needs all on your own. Well, you can, but it will be a lot more difficult while you take a tiny baby around with you. I've had tons of experience with babies so here I am. We need to call a truce as much as we can and focus on Doe, okay?"

Several seconds pass.

"Okay. I can't guarantee I'm not going to carry on insulting you."

"I'm definitely going to be giving you grief."

"That's okay then. I accept and appreciate your offer of help."

"Now that's out of the way, I'll show you what I've brought. But first why don't you make me a coffee, go and get dressed and I'll cuddle Doe while you do so."

He hands his daughter to me and I want to cry. She's so damn precious. Her tiny, warm body fits into my arms and I sit back on the sofa and just stare over every inch of her. Those cherubic cheeks, her little rosebud mouth, the smattering of dark hair on her head and her dark eyebrows. I can't help it; I lean in and take a sniff of her head. The smell of babies is irresistible.

"Did you seriously just sniff my kid?" Scott's looking at me with a furrowed brow as he holds my steaming hot cup of coffee in his hand.

"I did. She smells gorgeous."

His face changes to an expression of pride. "Yeah, she does, doesn't she? Right, I'll put this on this shelf up here. Don't drink it holding Doe, will you? You might spill it on her."

"Fucking hell. Scott Sullivan showing concern for a member of the female species. All it took was for them to be a couple of months old."

"I'm going to get dressed."

"Grab a shower if you want. It could be awhile before you get another one." I shout after him.

"Okay, thanks." He shouts back.

I settle back and spend the next twenty minutes or so just staring at this little sleeping girl in my arms.

WHEN SCOTT RETURNS, his hair is now damp and remains dishevelled. I don't like what's happening right now because he's looking all hot daddy. I might actually punch myself in the face in a minute. I reckon it's a biological physiological response. I'm sitting with a baby and so it's set something off inside me where I'm now looking at the nearest male to me like they're a potential father to my children.

Jesus, I don't know if I can do this.

I fucking detest this guy. I can't be having pathetic thoughts because Doe is setting off my maternal instincts. Perhaps I'd be better just showing him the stuff I've bought and then leaving? Yep, that's what I'll do. Give him my purchases, give him some pointers on childcare and then leave him to it.

"Hey, Suki. When do babies eat normal food? Can she have some whizzed up spag bol for lunch?"

Fuck, no way can I leave.

Holding out Doe to her father, extremely reluctantly I might add, I stand up, have a swig of coffee and then drag my bags closer to the sofa. I kneel down on his carpet near the bags and begin to take things out.

"Okay, firstly. I bought one of these bouncing seats for little babies. You can get better versions than this, but it was all I could carry and they're great for right now when baby is awake in the daytime." I set it all up and then taking Doe I slide her onto it. "See now because of its tilted angle she's no longer laid down."

"I like it."

I reach back into another bag. "Two books.

One about general childcare and another about weaning and first foods. You have homework and that's to read these books so that you know more about your current situation."

He grabs those off me with gusto. "Thank fuck. This is what I need. Some kind of manual for looking after a kid."

I reach into the third bag. "Bath wash, a baby towel, comb, nail clippers etc. I thought we'd give Doe her first bath."

"She'll drown in my big bath. She's only tiny."

"Give me a minute."

I walk into his kitchen and sure enough he has a washing-up bowl. It's square and grey. I carry it out back into his living room.

"You want me to put my daughter where I put my dirty plates?"

I laugh. "It's perfect for her. I'll show you in a minute. But first let me get the stuff out of this last bag."

From the fourth bag I bring out romper suits, cute little outfits, tights, and all manner of other clothing. I already bought her a few bits of clothing yesterday, but today I had more time to peruse and I couldn't resist buying more.

"I must owe you about a million pounds."

"You don't owe me anything. They're all presents for Doe."

"Are you one of those secret millionaires I've seen on TV?"

I laugh. "No, just a sucker for a cute baby."

He looks at Doe. "Yeah, me too it would seem. Who knew?"

I START REMOVING tags from the clothes. "Ideally these should be washed first, but we'll put her in one after her bath and then we can do a washload later. You'll need to buy some sensitive skin wash powder."

"I already have that. Anything else makes me feel like I have fleas. That's actually one thing I can manage, hurrah. I can put a load on. I even know how to sort colours, Suki."

"Bloody hell, Scott. I'm discovering you have hidden depths. I only knew you were good at removing female clothing, not actually washing them. In a bit I'll even get to see you putting women's clothes back on. Miracles are occurring today."

"Finish your drink and shut up. I'm going to

wash the mountain of pink you've bought, and then we can do this bath."

To one side I put some pink leggings, pink socks, and a white t-shirt that says 'I love my Daddy' on it in pink letters. I deliberately don't show Scott it. I add a sleeveless vest to the pile and spotting an open packet of nappies next to the sofa arm, one of those too. I add the baby wash and baby towel to the pile.

"So let me show you the bathroom." Scott says when he comes back in.

"No need. We can do it right here." I stand up. "I'll just fill this bowl up with warm water. Do you have a large towel you can put on the carpet?" He nods and we both leave the room going off in different directions.

"So just put her in like this." I show Scott how to place her in the bowl. "You see, it's the perfect fit for tiny babies. It makes them feel secure. You can get a baby bath for when she's bigger. We should write a list and go shopping today while I'm here. I can help you carry stuff. Although," I pause. "I guess you shouldn't buy too much in case her mum comes back."

At this, Scott's jaw sets and his eyes narrow and seem to darken beyond their original chocolate depths. "She can come back. She's not having Doe. I'll fight her in court. I don't need a DNA test because it's clear she's my child, but tomorrow I'll be taking legal advice. No mother who abandoned her daughter without a forwarding address or even any baby equipment, not even a clean nappy, is taking my child. No. Fucking. Way."

Jesus. His macho protection of his daughter is making my nipples hard. I need to get out of here. I'm getting baby brain and I didn't even birth the baby.

We flick Doe with the warm water and she's now awake, those gorgeous huge eyes open. Scott's eyes take on something I've never seen before. Pride. "She's so gorgeous, isn't she, Suki? Am I biased because she's mine? I think she's the most beautiful thing I've ever seen."

"Well, you might be biased, but she is absolutely gorgeous." If his female admirers could see Scott now, they'd be green with envy as he looks at his daughter just how I imagine every one of his fan club would want him to look at them.

I help him lift her out and arrange the baby towel on her. "Make sure you dry every nook and cranny. I'll go empty this water out. Which way is the bathroom?"

He tells me and I leave him to it.

When I return, he's finished drying Doe and is putting a fresh nappy on her. "Jenson gave me the week off. First thing tomorrow I'm sorting out the doctor's appointment. I need that DNA test straight away. That and to see a solicitor."

"He's told me I can have time off too if you need me."

Scott looks up shocked. "But InHale is so busy. Plus," he gestures from him to me. "Why he thought that would be a good idea…"

"We've managed so far today, and the fact remains that no matter how much I think you're a complete dickhead, I can see you're fiercely protective already of the child you only met yesterday and I can deal with Scott, the father."

He tilts his head staring at me. "Yeah, I can deal with Suki, the helpful person with baby knowledge. As long as stuck up Suki from the bar doesn't turn up, I could use your help."

"It's just for Doe. She has to be the priority and she's better if I help you. Once you're on your feet I can back off and leave you to it."

"I reckon you'll only need to stay a couple of days."

I almost choke on my own saliva. "Stay?"

"You can't do a shift on the care of a baby, can you? I need twenty-four-hour round-the-clock observations here so Doe stays alive. Yes." He nods his head so hard I think it may actually bounce off. "The more I think about it, it's the best idea. I'll learn faster so you can fuck off faster. Suki, we need to go to yours so you can grab some things. You need to move in for a few days."

Usually when Scott talks, I have a sassy retort ready to fire back. This time I have nothing.

Not one word.

CHAPTER SEVEN

Scott

I stare at Suki as she agrees that we should go and get her stuff, and panic. I wasn't expecting her to say yes. I was half joking... I think.

Doe and I managed to survive last night. I'm sure I could cope now I've got the basics down, but as Suki's eyes drift down to Doe who's falling asleep in my arms after the excitement of her bath, I can't help but think that her being here just for a couple of days is for the best. I know single parents do this kind of thing every day, but they usually have a little heads up to do the research, read the book, create a nursery. *Fuck.*

"She doesn't even have a bedroom."

"She doesn't need one yet. She's better off with you for a while. If anything, it makes feeding easier. But there's no harm in looking for a bigger, maybe ground floor place I guess."

"Oh, I don't need a bigger place. This is a two-bedroomed flat."

"So what's wrong with the other bedroom then?"

"It's... uh... not exactly habitable."

"What's that meant to mean?"

"It's just a mess. I've never actually lived with anyone before and I'm not very good at tidying up after myself."

"It's not so bad," she says looking around my living area.

"I had a tidy up when we got home yesterday."

"Where's the room? I need to see what we're dealing with."

"Down the hall on the right."

She puts her coffee down and follows my directions. My eyes drop as she moves. She's wearing a pair of skin-tight jeans and the way her arse swings as she walks, well... fuck.

I swallow down the trickle of desire that threatens to emerge and remind myself that it's Suki I'm looking at. The badass bitch who hates my guts. There's only one reason she's here right now and that's the little lady in my arms. I need to remember that it's got fuck all to do with me.

"Fucking hell, Scott. Do I need to sign you up for Hoarders Anonymous?"

I groan. "It's just my storage room."

"For what?" she asks stepping back into the room. "All the shit you should have thrown away years ago?"

"Some of it, yeah, probably. But there's some useful stuff amongst it all. Plus... some sentimental stuff."

"I'm sorry, what? Did you say sentimental? Do you actually know what that word means?"

"Fuck you, Suki. I'm not actually the cold-hearted arsehole you make me out to be."

"Okay, prove it."

"P- prove it?" I stutter, not liking where this is going.

"Yeah, tell me something real. Something that will help me see the 'real' you that you're so adamant exists."

My heart races and I swallow nervously as I consider what I might be willing to give her.

I open and close my mouth a couple of times as a few options run through my head but in the end I go with one that she might be able to sympathise with easier.

"My mum…" I blow out a slow breath. I don't talk about this ever, especially with people I hate. "My mum died when I was nineteen. I held her hand and watched her leave me." A huge lump forms in my throat and I almost have to stop halfway through the sentence, unable to squeeze words past it.

"Shit, Scott. That's rough. I'm sorry."

I shrug. It is what it is. Not much I can do about it now.

"Your turn."

She pales. I'm guessing she wasn't expecting me to turn that onto her, but I've seen a different side to her the past two days and I'm starting to believe her outer bitch layer might be a little on the fake side.

"I was Doe."

"Weird coincidence. Why did you change your name?"

"It wasn't my name, arsewipe. I was her. I was the abandoned baby no one wanted."

My jaw drops. I stare at her. Her eyes harden, her lips press into a thin line as she builds her walls back up after that admission.

"I... uh..."

"Don't apologise. It's not like you were the one who abandoned me. You might have fucked every woman with a pulse, but I think you might have been too young to have been involved."

"I wasn't—" she raises an eyebrow at me. "Okay, so maybe I was."

Suddenly, everything she's done for Doe and me makes total sense. Her reason for putting aside everything she feels for me, or doesn't, becomes clear. This really is about Doe.

She sits back on the sofa, crosses her arms across her chest and stares at the black TV screen. It's clear she wants to talk about her past about as much as I do, and I fight to find a different topic of conversation.

"You know, there is one woman with a pulse I've not fucked."

"Oh yeah, who? The Queen?"

"Okay, make that two then. No, I was more thinking..." I drop my eyes to her tits that are pushing up over the top of her shirt with the way she's sitting.

"I don't fucking think so." She stands up and marches to the other side of the room, her face turning back into the sour one I'm used to when she turns her eyes on me. "You don't want my help, just say the word and the truce is over."

"No, no," I say in panic. "I want you here. I'm sorry, I was just... trying to change the subject away from the heavy stuff. I don't actually want to fuck you. The opposite actually."

Her brow furrows. "And what exactly is the opposite?"

"Uh... no idea. Shall we go out then?"

"You're an idiot."

"You wouldn't have me any other way."

"You sure about that?"

She shakes her head and starts packing a bag for Doe.

I can't help but smile as I think about how much fun the next few days could be.

―――――

IT TAKES FUCKING FOREVER to actually get out of the house. Just as we've about packed up everything that Doe owns, she grumbles because she wants another bottle. It's over an hour later when the three of us do eventually step over the threshold and into the hallway.

The second we're in the Uber, Suki pulls her phone from her pocket and puts it to her ear.

I can't hear what's being said on the other end but it's immediately obvious that it's a man. Something stirs inside me. I always assumed that Suki was single. I mean, what man in their right mind would put up with her brand of bitch for any length of time?

"Ha, well they're both still alive if that's what you mean." She glances over at both of us, making it even more obvious that she's talking about me. "I know right?" She laughs and my spine stiffens. Are they laughing at me? I start to fume but I'm cut off with the next words out of her mouth. "Listen, I need a favour. Well... Scott needs a favour. His spare room isn't exactly fit for purpose. Any chance you'd be up for fixing up a nursery?"

They chat away for a little longer, allowing me to stew on what they're planning for my flat and daughter and not filling me in on.

She eventually hangs up. "Okay, that's sorted."

"What's sorted? What have you done?"

"That was my cousin, Carl. He's a builder. He's going to come around and help out with the nursery, or should I say tip. He's going to—"

"I'm more than capable of sorting out my own daughter's nursery," I snap, but when her face drops, I immediately feel bad. She's just trying to do something nice.

"I- I know that. But you've got enough on your hands; you don't need more adding to it. I'm sorry. If you don't want—"

"No. I'm sorry. I need all the help I can get."

She turns and looks out of the window. I'm assuming I'm not meant to hear the words that pass her lips. "Wow, he does know how to apologise."

I open my mouth to respond, but concerned we'll just end up in a slanging match before we've even started our few days together, I shut it again and turn to face my sleeping daughter.

"What's first on the list?" I ask once we're standing in the retail park Suki directed the driver to.

She looks me up and down, standing with a carrier bag full of Doe's stuff in one hand and her in her car seat in the other. "Pushchair and nappy bag."

"Pushchair it is. I looked at them when my

auntie sent me out yesterday. I actually had some help from the shop assistant and I already know the one I want... I think."

I march straight into the shop and locate the one I was test running yesterday. It's a different colour to what I saw yesterday, and it throws me a bit, but I come to a stop next to it and announce, "This one."

"Er... that was quick."

"You want to know why?" She stares at me curiously so I put Doe down, and make quick work of unclipping the seat that's currently on the frame before slotting Doe's car seat into place.

"Wow. I'm impressed, Daddy."

"Hmmm... it's weird."

"Why's that?"

"I've only ever been referred to as that in the bedroom. Sounds all kinds of wrong out in public."

"There's something seriously wrong with you." She rolls her eyes as a shop assistant walks over and starts to give us the speech about the pushchair before I stop her midflow by announcing that I want it, but in navy, not black.

"And does Mummy agree with this choice?" the woman asks turning to Suki. I follow her stare to find the most horrified look on Suki's face.

"Oh, no, no, no. She's not... I'm not..."

"Oh God, I- I'm so sorry."

The shop assistant tells us she'll get everything sorted and leave our details behind the till before running off with a tomato-red face.

"That was fun. Let's see who else we can freak out," Suki suggests rubbing her hands together.

"And you think I'm the one with issues."

"THIS IS INSANE," I mutter, looking at the amount of stuff we've bought, and it's only the tip of the iceberg seeing as all the big stuff is going to be delivered over the coming days.

I pull out a bank card that I hardly ever use and hand it over, fully expecting it to be rejected. But thankfully it goes through and I breathe a sigh of relief. After I sold Mum's house, I put everything that I inherited into a bank account and left it there for a rainy day. I knew that at some point in my future I'd need it, whether to settle down myself or... I guess, ready for the day a random woman dropped my surprise daughter with me and ran. Emotion burns the back of my eyes as I think about what an incredible grandmother my mum would have been. She'd be in her element if she was still here now.

I don't say anything but somehow Suki must sense the change in me. She reaches over and squeezes my hand. "She's going to love all this." I've no idea if she's talking about Doe or what my mum would have thought but having someone beside me right now does make me feel a little better.

CHAPTER EIGHT

Suki

"Come on, let's get everything in the Uber and then just pop to mine quickly for me to get a few things. Then we can go to yours and get settled for the night."

Scott looked a bit emotional and although I wouldn't have believed he was capable, having a baby daughter almost literally dropped on your lap would overwhelm anyone. I wonder if he was thinking of his mum then and what she'd have thought to having a granddaughter? He's not mentioned a father and although I'm intrigued, I'm not asking, as he might want me to share something else about my own past and me and Scott Sullivan do not confide in each other, we slag each other off. That's our thing.

He waits in the Uber while I go into my own flat and pack stuff for a couple of days. I make sure to stick an extra couple of changes of outfit in my duffle in case of baby sick, piss, or shit. Better to be prepared. Before long we're on our way back to Scott's place.

"Thanks for this, Suki. Really." Scott says after a few minutes of silence. "I think what's happened is just starting to sink in. Yesterday and this morning, I've been so busy and shocked that I've just got on with things, but now, coming back and facing a second night at home with Doe, it's hitting me. It's real, isn't it? I have a daughter."

His eyes stare into mine and there's a rawness there I've never seen before. Worryingly, it makes me want to reach out my arms and comfort him. Thank fuck my arms are weighted down with belongings and I'm strapped in.

"It is real, and it's going to take some time for it to truly sink in. I think once the DNA test is done, that'll be a load off because as much as she looks your double, you just can't be definite, can you?"

"When you gave me Doe yesterday, if you'd have done a DNA test and she wasn't mine, I'd have shouted 'hallelujah' and probably booked a vasectomy. But now," he swallows. "If they say she's not mine, I think I'll actually die. I don't know what's happening to me, Suki. Can you have a go at me because I need some normality to centre me right now."

"It's about time something happened to make you grow up because you're a manslut, and now I've seen your spare room, I can confirm you're a dirty, filthy manslut."

"That's why the ladies love me." He winks.

"They'd not love the diseases that come with you. If you don't give them the clap, they might get some kind of fungus from that place."

"Hey, I'm clean. I get checked. And I always wrap it."

"Well I guess it's a bonus you put some of your shit in a plastic bag."

"You're calling my dick shit? Just shows that you're woefully ignorant of what it can do."

I look pointedly at Doe in her car seat, eyes open. "Oh I can see what it can do. Guess some plastic bags have holes in, maybe?"

If he doesn't actually beam. "Good though, isn't she?"

Laughing, I nudge his arm. "Can't disagree with that one actually."

"Thanks for the banter. I feel better now. More normal." He says as the Uber pulls up outside his place.

"Yeah, you'll not be saying that in a minute when we're trying to assemble baby paraphernalia."

When we get into the flat, I close the curtains while Scott feeds Doe, changes her nappy and puts her a vest on. I purchased a sleeping bag and I put her in it. "See, she doesn't need covers now. It keeps her snuggly all night."

"And she looks even fucking cuter and I didn't think that was possible." Scott says kissing her head. Seriously, the guy's had a personality transplant. I'm actually looking for his secret twin or evidence of a brain injury.

"Now she just needs a cot to sleep in." I announce.

Scott groans.

After an hour-and-a-half, the cot is done and so is Scott. I'd taken Doe out of the Grobag as the cot glue wouldn't be dry tonight and I'd dressed her in a sleepsuit and put her in her Moses basket. I walk over to my bag and pull out a four pack of beer.

"Celebration drink?"

"You had beer all the time I was making that fuckarse of a cot and kept quiet? I may never forgive you."

"You needed to be able to fully concentrate on the instructions. Now you deserve one, or two if you like. I'll stick to one."

He reaches a hand out for a can. I hand it to him. "Yeah, I'd better just have one seeing as I'm now a responsible adult."

I've just taken a drink out of my own can and at his words I spray a whole mouthful of beer directly into his face.

"Was that entirely necessary?"

"A responsible adult. Hahahahahaha. If you were a responsible adult, she wouldn't be in there would she?"

He placed a hand on his hip. "I'm obviously super fertile and somehow one escaped."

That has me in hysterics again. "Scott Sullivan Sperm Olympics." I shout out.

"Oh fuck off." Is all he can manage to come back with.

SCOTT OFFERED to sleep on the sofa with Doe at the side of him but of course I wouldn't hear of it. "No, you need to get settled into a routine. Anyway, I'm nearer the kitchen here. I can make myself a drink. Hopefully, you'll manage through the night and I'll realise I'm not needed.

Scott bids me a goodnight and once he's left, I change into my pyjamas, lie on the sofa, rest my head on the pillow I brought from home and pull the sheets over me that Scott supplied. I start to think about the sofa. I hope it's not been the scene of a thousand Scott shagfests. The thought makes me feel a bit ill and I rearrange myself so that I'm lying on one sheet with the others on top of me, even though I'd been sitting on the sofa happily all night. The mind does weird things in an evening when it has time on its hands.

Scott must only have been in bed an hour and I don't know if he's been asleep, but I haven't when Doe lets out a shriek of a cry. It's not like her previous cries for food and so I dash towards Scott's room. I knock and he shouts, "Come in."

Rushing into the room, Scott's bedside lamp is on and he's walking around the bedroom with Doe in his arms. She's sobbing her heart out and screaming, her face beet-red and scrunched up. "What's the matter with her, Suki? She seems in pain. Should I phone an ambulance?"

I hate seeing the little beauty in pain but know it's unlikely to be serious. "Let's do the usual things. Change her nappy first. Then give her a bottle."

As we change her nappy, Doe pulls her knees up to her chest, crying all the time. Scott looks about to join her. I send him to make her bottle but she refuses it when I try to give it her.

Scott is pacing and hysterical. "She's dying, Suki. Dying. I'm going to call 999. Fuck, I can't live without her. Don't die, Doe, please. Can you dial 999 while I pray?" He drops to his knees. I place Doe on the bed for a second and I do something I've wanted to do for a long, long time. I slap Scott's face.

He looks at me wide-eyed. His hand to his smarting cheek.

"W- what did you do that for?"

"Get a grip. She's probably got colic. Unfortunately, we forgot to buy some colic medicine."

"What's colic?"

"I dunno really but something babies get regularly and it's really painful. I'll be right back." I run and get my phone, bringing up a web page and searching for colic. When I return, Scott is walking around with a still wailing Doe, looking even more panicked.

"Okay it suggests a warm bath can help, so let's get that organised and I'll pop out to the supermarket for some colic medicine."

"You really think it's colic and we don't need an ambulance?"

"I really do. She's doing everything it says. Her grimacing and pulling her knees up. I'll go fill the washing up bowl."

"No. I have it in hand. Can you get dressed and get the medicine please as soon as possible?"

"Okay." I leave the room and start getting ready.

I hear Scott go into the bathroom and once dressed I go to see what he's doing given I thought Doe was being bathed in the bowl for now. Walking into the bathroom, I witness Doe laid in a pile of soft towels on the floor, while Scott strips off entirely butt naked.

My hand immediately goes up in front of my

eyes. "Whoa, whoa, whoa, whoa, whoa. What the fuck is happening here?"

"I'm getting in the bath with Doe. Then I can hold her in the water and cuddle her, so she knows she's safe and protected."

"My eyes weren't fucking protected."

"It's a dick, Suki. Haven't you seen one before?"

"You're a dick." I shout. "I'm off to buy the colic stuff."

I walk out of the bathroom, dropping my hand from my eyes, and then for reasons I cannot explain, I look through the crack in the bathroom door. I tell myself I'm checking that Scott gets safely in the bath without dropping the baby, but all I really notice is a mighty fine arse, taut and muscled thighs that I imagine feel like rock as I watch him lower himself carefully into the tub, and his dick swinging proudly from side to side before he's submerged under the water. He then coos at Doe as he cuddles her.

"Come on, baby. Don't cry. Come on, Daddy doesn't like it."

That breaks my stupor. The faster I get to the supermarket, the faster Doe gets her colic treatment. I grab my bag and more or less run out of the door, away from the frantic father trying to console his baby and away from that pretty impressive package that my brain needs to block out.

***

I GET a weird look in the supermarket when I smack myself in the forehead, but the vision of Scott's dick won't leave and I can't cope. Now I know why women try to come back for more, especially if he knows what to do with it, and given his fan club he must do. I buy some colic medicine, a few other medicine type things that could come in handy like Savlon, a thermometer because we need to check her temp and make sure it definitely is colic, and then I quickly go and grab a punnet of cherries because I need some comfort food.

Dashing back to the flat, I let myself in and go back to the bathroom. Ignoring Scott's nakedness, I read the instructions and give Doe a dropper of the colic liquid.

"Has she been any better?" I attempt to ask over the screaming.

"I think the warm water has helped. She stops for a minute but then starts again."

"Well, we just need to wait for the medicine to kick in and then hopefully she'll be okay. If it is colic the instructions say you can give it with every feed. Oh and I got a thermometer. Not the basic kind. An all singing, all dancing one. So we can make sure she's okay."

We sit in the bathroom for the next twenty minutes and eventually, Doe's sobs subside and her eyes begin to close. Scott passes her to me and I turn around and dry her while he gets out of the bath. Placing her carefully onto the pile of towels once more so Scott can pick her up when dressed, I start to back out of the room.

"It's okay, I have a towel on." Scott says and so I slowly turn around.

"Thank God, she's stopped crying. I have to admit I was starting to panic." I confess.

"You were like the coolest person on the planet while I just fell to pieces."

"No, I wasn't. I just wanted to try to keep you calm."

Carefully stepping around a now sleeping Doe, Scott hugs me. His towel is only wrapped around his waist and so his wet chest soaks into my t-shirt. However, I allow him a hug, the man must need it.

"Well, let's try to get some sleep now because

tomorrow you need to make the doctor's appointment and then we need to tackle emptying your spare room ready for Carl coming." I say, breaking the hug and stepping away.

Scott nods but he seems distracted. "Nice rack." He says.

I look at the towel rack and think it's a strange thing to come out with, but he has just had a shock. "Erm, yeah. Is it heated?"

"You tell me." He says and winks, and then I realise. Looking down, I see the wet from his chest has soaked through my wet t-shirt and my nipples are standing proud.

"You're a fucking pig." I yell.

"Sshh, don't wake the baby." He says, laughing as I stomp from the room.

CHAPTER NINE

Scott

As I lie in bed listening to Doe's soft breathing beside me, only one image plays out in my mind. Suki's tits.

I've had two nights without sex. Two. And one look at a pair of tits and it's all I can think about. It doesn't matter that on a normal day I wouldn't touch the woman they're attached to with a barge pole. But I can't help the allure of a nice full pair. My cock stirs to life as I think about her rosy-pink nipples clearly visible through her top.

I allow my imagination to run away with me

for a few minutes before Doe stirs and a stark realisation hits me.

I'm never going to get laid again.

How can I when I'm a full-time parent? I can hardly take her with me.

My frustration with the situation only lasts so long before Doe starts to whimper and I drag my body from the bed so I can prepare her bottle before she really starts to complain.

I don't bother putting the lights on. I just rely on my torch on my phone to allow me to see enough to prep the bottle so that I don't wake Suki. I'm not sure when I started being concerned enough about her to allow her to sleep. I tell myself that it's just because if she were to wake, all I'd see is her tits again and that's not good for either of us.

I need to remember why she's here. And it's not for me.

She doesn't make a sound behind me, so I assume she's still sleeping, but when I turn around to make my way back to Doe, rolling her warm bottle between my palms, I find Suki staring right at me.

My movements stop the second our eyes connect. The image of her breasts that I've been trying to banish from my mind slams into me once again and I imagine she's laid there waiting for me. My cock swells with my need for a release. My teeth sink into my bottom lip as my brain shuts itself off and I take a step forward.

Suki's fingers tighten around the sheets that are around her waist and her eyes widen, but I don't register, my body moves of its own accord. I'm almost in touching distance when everything comes crashing down. Doe's cry fills the flat and I freeze.

I stare down at Suki, whose chest is heaving, with desire or fear I've no clue, but seeing as the situation is what it is, I can't imagine it's a positive response to my approach.

"Fuck," I grunt, lifting my free hand to my hair. *What the fuck was that?*

I race from the room almost as fast as I entered and push my bedroom door closed behind me in the hope it'll cut me off from what just happened.

It's the sleep deprivation, I tell myself. I'm just acting crazy and given how my life has changed in the last two days, that shouldn't really be a surprise. I've just realised that I'm probably never going to have sex again and I'm seeing her body as a different entity to her personality. I'm sure she'll give me some shit first thing in the morning, and I'll remember exactly why I hate her.

I give Doe her bottle and tuck her up onto my shoulder, resting my cheek against the top of her head and tap her back until she burps.

THE NEXT THING I KNOW, the morning sun is pouring through the edges of the curtains and I'm curled up in bed.

Doe. I sit up in a panic, thinking that I fell asleep with her on my chest and that I've rolled over and crushed her. My heart pounds against my ribs as I look around the bed for her little body.

She's not there.

A soft sigh comes from next to me and when I glance into her basket, she's in there sleeping soundly with a little bunny stuffed toy that Suki bought tucked into the crook of her arm. The relief I feel knowing she's safe is more than I can begin to describe.

Did I put her back but not remember?

I chastise myself for being so irresponsible and quietly climb from the bed, still feeling shaken up from what I could have done to my daughter.

I make use of the bathroom before heading out to the living room to find out what kind of mood Suki might be in. But when I get there, what was her bed has been turned back to a sofa, the sheets folded neatly on one of the seats and her stuff gone. Turning to the kitchen, I also find that empty.

What the fuck? I know I kinda stalked towards her last night like I was starving and she was my prey, but leaving seems a little extreme.

Falling down onto the sofa, I beat myself up for fucking this up. She was here helping, she didn't even have to step foot in this flat, let alone be here to support me.

I'm such a fucking idiot.

My eyes drop to the coffee table and I find a folded piece of paper sitting on the top with my name on.

Plucking it from its resting place, I suck in a deep breath, preparing for what she could possibly need to say to me in the form of a letter instead of in person.

Scott,

You both looked too peaceful to wake. I thought it was important that the two of you spend some time

*alone. Book a doctor's appointment, take her out for
a walk or something. Bond.*
You've got this, Daddy.
Suki.

My hand trembles. She's left? And without even saying goodbye.

I look back to my bedroom where Doe sleeps. I get that she could leave without saying anything to me, but Doe means more to her than she even wants me to see. How could she leave without saying goodbye to her?

My chest aches as I think about the women in Doe's life constantly turning their backs on her. I thought Suki wanted to make up for what she'd experienced, yet she runs at my first little fuck up.

Maybe she's not just the bitch I know her to be. She's a fucking pussy too.

Anger swirls around in me as I make the most of my still sleeping baby and have the quickest shower of my life. The second I turn the water off, I grab a towel and run towards the bedroom to make sure she's not fallen out or something.

Her big brown eyes turn my way when I step into the room and her lips curl up into a smile.

"Good morning, baby girl. Did you sleep

well?" I coo at her, my heart constricting for a whole other reason when she looks at me like I'm the most important person in her world.

Wrapping the towel around my waist, I scoop her up and cuddle her to my chest, breathing in her incredible baby scent.

"Looks like it's just the two of us today, sweet pea. What do you fancy doing?"

She makes some cute little noises as I walk us through to the living room and place her in her bouncer so I can make her bottle.

I turn the radio on so we've both got something to listen to and set about my new normal morning routine. Never in a million years did I think that would ever involve bottle prep but there we go. I would say stranger things have happened, but I don't really think they have.

I phone the doctors surgery the second they open and after a small argument with the woman on reception and having to briefly explain the situation, she finally caves and gives me an appointment for two hours time. I've no idea how long it might take the two of us to get ready and get out of here so I can only hope and pray that we don't miss it.

With Doe dressed in a pretty pink dress and

bundled up in her polar bear outfit, the two of us step from the flat. I've got her in one arm and the folded pushchair in the other.

I've no idea how I'm going to manage this, but I figured anything was better than bouncing her down the stairs.

By some freaking miracle, I manage to open the frame with just one hand and my foot, and keep Doe safely tucked in my arm. In mere minutes Doe is safely strapped in with a blanket tucked around her. I smile at myself for how seamless it was, but when I look up, I find a couple of young women sitting on a bench a few feet away with amused smirks on their faces. Usually at seeing them, I'd march right over and find out what about me had them so interested, but right now the only girl in my mind is the one who's ready to go exploring the big city.

"Come on then, let's go and find that doctor, hey?"

She coos and we set off on the short walk to the surgery.

We arrive right on time and thankfully aren't forced to wait too long. I was proud of myself for remembering to bring everything Doe might need in case we ended up spending the rest of the morning sitting here waiting, but when my name's called to go through I've not had to touch any of it.

The doctor's lovely. She listens as if she's not got a waiting roomful of other patients to see and does a thorough check of all Doe's vitals just to be sure that's she's healthy. Much to my relief she's happy with everything and with all the information I need to go about getting a DNA test, we head off home.

I give Doe her bottle and get us both settled before getting online and reading up more on paternity tests, something I probably should have done before going to the doctors but I've not exactly been firing on all cylinders the past couple of days.

I'm just reading through how to get a test when my phone pings with a message.

Sarah: Hey, how's it going?

Since we reconnected after my bumping into her at Inhale around eighteen months ago, we've become pretty good friends. Her guy, Emmett, can even look at me now like I'm not trying to steal his woman. I'd broken her heart when we were teenagers but she realises now that I was a horny teenage boy with family problems and I couldn't do much about my abrupt departure from her life as I was carted off to hospital to get my head checked.

Me: It's going...

I snap a photo of Doe and send it. Not two seconds later, she's calling.

"Please don't tell me you've started cradle-snatching now?"

"Nah, I've always gone for older over younger if I'm honest."

"Ugh, such a pig. So whose is she?"

"Mine," I state proudly.

"Fuck off. You banging her mum or something?"

"Yeah, apparently I did, like eleven months ago," I can't help my own joke.

"Scott," she warns. "You're worrying me. Please tell me you're joking."

"Deadly serious. Deadly."

"You've got a fucking kid?" she screeches, making me pull the phone from my ear.

"Ssh, she might hear you."

"I don't even know where to start."

I fill Sarah in on the basics of my weekend,

much to her horror. She's a nanny, so a kid's safety is a number one priority to her.

"Do you need me to come over? I've got the twins, but if you need me then—"

"We're going okay. Suki's been here helping." My stomach gets heavy at the mention of her name. I've managed to ignore the fact she upped and left this morning without a word, but it hits me upside the head once again.

"Suki? Sarah asks sceptically.

"Don't worry, you can be as shocked by the whole situation as me."

"Wow, just wow, Scott. Is there anything you do need?"

We chat for a while longer and she agrees to pull together some stuff for me, before the twins need her attention. We say our goodbyes and when I look to Doe, she's out cold.

I guess there's no time like the present to start on her bedroom. Pushing the door open, I assess the situation and set to work.

CHAPTER TEN

Suki

I'm out of here.

After the stress of Doe and her colic last night, he stared at my breasts like he'd never seen any before. Then this morning, well, I don't know what that was all about, but it's uncomfortable territory. We're not even friends, never mind anything else. So, I decided to come back to my own place, grab a shower and go back to work. I'm on a shift from midday until nine pm and I'll think about whether I call and offer to sleep on the sofa again or not while I'm at work. I want some normality.

Jenson sounded surprised when I rang to tell him I was coming in as normal. I just told him Scott seemed to have a plan, which he did. I'd no intention of going to the doctors with him and I'm sure he can push a pram around the park on his own. Basically, I need to get it into my own thick head that this baby is nothing to do with me and let him get on with it.

I start to wipe down the bar and get everything ready, but my mind keeps straying back to Doe. How heart-breaking it was when she was in pain. The sheer helplessness that came with trying to look after her. Surely I cried and looked like that when I was a baby, but it hadn't been enough for my family to want to keep me either.

I wish we knew something about Doe's mum, so I could reach out. I could see if she was just needing help. I mean what if she's in a bad way? How can Scott not even know her name? It just shows what a pig of a human being he is when he sticks in dick in women and doesn't even know what they're called. He can't tell you who his baby mama is and where she might live. Appalling, that's what it is.

"What's the cloth done to offend you?"

Chester, who's on shift with me asks. I look down and see I have it clenched in my hand like I'm strangling it. "You imagining it's Scott's neck?"

"How d'you guess?" I laugh.

Chester is a student who works for us between his studying. He's tall and thin with soft blonde wavy hair and he attracts the younger women into the bar it has to be said. Luckily, he's what you'd call a nice boy, quite bashful, and goes bright red at Scott's suggestions of what he should do with interested parties.

"I can totally believe he has a kid, as in fathered one. I'm actually surprised it's just one. But being left to look after it." He shakes his head. "That I can't imagine. Finally, a woman to bring him to his knees, even if it's just to change a nappy."

I burst out laughing. This is what we do at InHale. We banter, we mostly all get along, and our shifts pass fast because it's a great place to work.

It's a busy shift and I only get a brief chance to chat to Jenson who tells me that Leah has sorted out a pile of clothes, toys, etc that they no longer need. It looks like I need to go back to Scott's after my shift after all.

I head into the staff room on my short break and take out my phone to find I have two messages. One is from Carl who wonders how I've got on. I call him because it's easier and ask if he can pop to Scott's flat tomorrow evening. I'm off tomorrow anyway and although I should keep out of it all, I want to make sure Doe has everything she needs in that room, so I want to be there. *Just another couple of days*, I tell myself. Then I can get back to normal. My arms crave to hold Doe and to smell her baby smell. I'm hooked on a baby that's not mine. She's not even family to me. Maybe what the issue really is, is that I crave more family of my own. I know my personality can be a little, can we say, fiery, but underneath the ash I have a warm centre. It's just I've spent a lot of my life being rejected, so trusting people doesn't come easily.

I've had relationships in the past, but they've been largely just sexual. As soon as someone tries to get to know me more, my prickly barriers come back up and then they're gone. And I've told myself I'm fine. That I've managed years on my own and I can manage more, but Doe is already showing me that it's not true. That I do want more. I want my own child. Not now, but one day, and I want love. The love of a good man who can put up with my baggage and well, unpack me, I guess. Carl has offered to set me up before. I might consider it soon. I'll just get all this helping Scott out of the way first.

And that's who the second message is from. I open the text.

Scott: I'm so fucking tired, Suki. Where are you?

I begin to type

Suki: I'm at work.

Scott: But Jenson gave you time off to help me?

Suki: You don't need my help.

Scott: Yes, actually, I do.

Suki: Did you go to the doctors?

Scott: Yes, she's in perfect health and I know what to do about the paternity test.

Suki: How's Doe now? Any colic again?

Scott: No, that colic stuff with a feed is working.

Suki: Then you don't need me.

Scott: I need to fucking sleep.

Suki: I'm not coming around just so you can sleep. That's just life with a baby.

There's a pause.

Scott: Well if I nod off and she rolls off the sofa, I did ask...

Suki: Oh FFS, I'll be round after my shift so about half ten. Also I'm off tomorrow and Carl is coming around to

**look at the room so I'll help you empty it
if you haven't done it already.**

**Scott: How can I have done it already?
Where did I put Doe, up my arse?**

Suki: Mr Wonderful can't multi-task?

**Scott: God you're a bitch. See you at
half ten.**

My mouth drops open. I'm a bitch but okay to
come around so he can sleep. And there was no
mention of the awkward moments from last night
and this morning. Christ, I bet he doesn't even
know he's doing it. Well, while I'm teaching him
about Doe, I think I'll give him a few words about
the treatment of women. Maybe, aahhh, yes... that
should do it. I think.

Now I'm looking forward to going back.

SCOTT LETS me back into his flat and to be fair
he does look absolutely knackered. After dropping

the bags from Leah in the hallway, I take Doe out of his hands. "Go get a shower, smelly boy... and some clean clothes."

"What's the point? They don't stay clean for long." He says, but he heads off to his room anyway. Outside his room he stops and turns to look at the bags on the floor. "Is that stuff to help me clean the room out? Like black plastic bags etc?"

"Nope. Leah sent a pile of stuff they don't need any longer."

He scrubs a hand through his hair. "Sarah says she's visiting and has some stuff too. I mean how much does a tiny baby need? We're supposed to be tidying up, but I'm being overrun."

"We can go through it all. I'm sure you don't need to keep everything, but babies keep growing and needing new things. We need to make sure Carl builds in good storage into Doe's room."

"I'm too tired to think about anything else. Seriously, I thought hangovers were bad, late nights from the pub or coming home in the early hours after servicing a woman, but fucking hell." I watch as he sways in the doorway. "It's got nothing on sleep deprivation due to a baby."

"I'll make some supper because I've brought

some leftovers from the restaurant in with this lot, and then I might let you go to bed."

"I didn't even get time to eat today, apart from a slice of bread. Didn't even have time to butter it, Suki. I mean what did I do all day? Right, I'm gonna get changed into a clean top." He goes into his bedroom. I take Doe into the living room and after some gorgeous snuggles I put her down and start reheating food.

My fun starts as Scott comes back into the living room. I pass him his food to rest on his lap and put a glass of water near him on the coffee table.

"I missed Doe today." I tell Scott truthfully.

"She's beautiful. I've not had a minute and now I have I can't stop staring at her. It's crazy."

"Yet in the blink of an eye she'll be at school and then she'll be dating."

I watch his face turn pale and he swallows. "Dating. No, I can't deal."

"You'll be having to vet them all for their suitability. Although... what if she's just in a bar some night and gets charmed by a random bartender who shags her, doesn't even ask her name and then fucks her off?"

His face is puce. "I'd fucking kill him. Oh my

fucking god." He gets up, pacing the living room. "How am I not dead, Suki? I've done this to so many women. Where are their father's? There might be a Facebook group. Angry fathers with pitchforks, coming to chop off my dick for what I've done to their daughters. I need a church, Suki. I need to repent."

I'm in fits watching his meltdown.

"She is not dating a 'me'. Over my dead body."

"Well, you might be dead if those pitchfork bearing dads come after you."

He sits on the sofa in shock. "I really have been a shit."

Just when I think I'm not only tormenting him but getting him to see his treatment of women is not the best he declares.

"I must remember to ask them their names, and maybe write it on the back of my hand, just until I get home."

"There's no hope. You really are a shit." I announce. "Now if you've eaten you might as well go to bed."

"Alone? Or are you offering? Only it's been a couple of days and I've got blue balls."

"Enough." I yell and then I look at Doe, thanking God I haven't just woken her up. "Scott. I can't do this here. I know at work we banter, but here I can't deal with it. This is a space for us to work together as best we can to look after Doe. If you're going to be staring at my soaked boobs, leering... well, it can't be good for Doe hearing me getting pissed off with you."

I'm shocked when I see Scott's shoulders slump. "I'm sorry, Suki. You're right. It's just... everything is changing and right now you're the only constant. You still detest me. You're here for Doe which I really appreciate. That's why I was trying to banter. That and well, I'm going to be honest. I'm a slut and I haven't had sex. I'm gagging for it."

"For God's sake, go to bed, have a wank, and get some sleep." I announce.

"You sound so romantic." He smirks.

"Go. Now. I'll talk to you in a few hours when Doe wakes us up for a feed." I tell him.

"Night, Suki," he says. Then he turns back.

"If you come kiss your daughter's head and wake her up, then you stay with her," I tell him straight.

"God, all right. Keep your hair on. If there's any down there."

"SCOTT."

"It's the last one, I promise." He chuckles as he leaves the room.

"Your daddy still has a lot to learn about us women, hasn't he, Doe?" I coo into the cot. "He needs a crash course in how to treat a lady."

CHAPTER ELEVEN

Scott

The sound of Doe's soft cries wakes me in the night, but the moment I hear Suki's soothing voice I almost instantly pass back out knowing that she's in safe hands. The last few days have completely drained me and I honestly don't know what I'd have done tonight if it wasn't for Suki. Never ever will I look at a mum again and judge her for not having washed her hair or for wearing clothes that are about two days past going in the washer. This shit is hard fucking work. I also understand why women do it time and time again without so much of a second thought because the look that brightens up Doe's face even when I so much as look at her is addictive as fuck. If I saw that every day for the rest of my life, then I'd die a seriously fucking happy man.

It wasn't just Doe that wiped me out though. While she was napping, I attempted to make some headway on the spare room in the hope that I wouldn't have to do some of it with Suki watching my every move. There's a very good reason why all that stuff is hidden behind that door; it's because I don't want to have to remember that time of my life and the pain that came along with it. But as much as I've wanted to forget, I've also never been able to get rid of the boxes of her stuff. It's always helped me feel connected to her even though she's been gone a long time now.

I feel so much better when I throw my legs over the edge of the bed the next morning. I've had almost a full night's sleep and I think I might be emotionally stable enough to do what needs to be done.

After a visit to the bathroom, I make my way into the living room to check on the girls. Suki is laid out on the sofa with a sleeping Doe curled up on her chest.

Assuming she's fallen asleep like it, I walk over to take Doe from her.

"It's okay, I'm awake," Suki whispers, scaring the shit out of me. "Just enjoying cuddle time."

I stare down at the two of them and something happens in my chest. It constricts, physically aches, at the sight. This is what Doe should have. Two loving parents. Yet it's something she's possibly never going to experience.

"A- Are you okay?" Suki's eyes scan my face. Fearing she can see too much, I turn and walk to the kitchen, announcing that I'm going to make coffee.

I hear movement behind me, but I don't turn to look at what she's doing.

Thankfully, the noise from the coffee machine drowns out some of the thoughts. I grab a couple of mugs and turn to get the milk, but before my eyes find the fridge, they land on Suki, who's standing in the doorway with her eyebrows knitted together and one of my hoodies pulled tightly around her.

"Are you sure you're okay? You seemed kind of manic last night, and this morning... well, you just look sad."

"I'm fine. The last few days are just taking their toll." I refuse to admit to her, or myself, that I'm afraid that things might get too much for me. I can't allow myself to go there because Doe needs at least one stable parent. My stress and anxiety right now need to take a backseat. It's controlled me once before and it's a time in my life I'd rather not revisit ever, but especially not when I've got a baby relying on me for everything.

"Okay, well if you need anything, you know where I am."

Plastering on my game face, I throw over my shoulder, "Anything?"

"Within reason, Mr Sullivan."

I turn just in time to see her bend over to run her fingers over Doe's cheek. The hoodie she's wearing rises up her thighs and gives me just a hint of her arse hiding beneath. I've always been an arse man and in those tight leggings I can't deny that Suki's is fine.

"I can feel you staring, Scott," she warns without looking my way.

"Of course I am, my daughter's beautiful."

She laughs but doesn't say any more.

"OKAY, she's fed, happy, and sleeping. Time to tackle that bedroom. You ready?" I swallow nervously. "Why are you scared? It's just a room full of crap."

I nod and rise from the sofa as she does. I refrain from telling her that it's not just crap. Depending on how the next few hours go she might just find out for herself how much some stuff in there means to me.

We clear out my gym equipment. Suki suggests that I put it all up for sale online seeing as it's covered in at least a year's worth of dust.

I agree and after giving it a wipe down, I snap a few photos before lining it all along the wall in my bedroom temporarily.

There are a couple of old suitcases, a bag of wrapping paper and some Christmas cards that have fallen out of their box that I had all good intentions about but never did anything with.

"Don't get me wrong, I just didn't really have you down as the kind of guy to decorate this place and to get into the Christmas spirit aside from some mistletoe action."

"You're right. They've not been put up in years."

"Awesome, something else that can go then."

"No," I say in a panic as she goes to put the box in the hallway.

"Okay?" She hesitates before placing it down behind her, eyeing me curiously.

"Doe will want it decorated when the time comes, I'm not buying it all again."

The truth is, that tree and all the boxes of decorations were my mums. Every year I'd sit excitedly at the top of the stairs while she climbed up into our attic to get everything down. We'd blast cheesy Christmas music as loud as we could and we'd decorate the entire house together. It was always my favourite time of year, until it became my worst.

"I guess you're right. We'll just need somewhere better to store it." I breathe a sigh of relief that she's bought my lie. I'm aware that if Doe does stay with me permanently, then Christmas is something that I'm going to have to learn to celebrate again. It suddenly seems like it might be so much easier to bear if I've got Doe's happy face helping me.

"Scott?" Suki asks, her voice lifting a tone or two as she rummages through a box. "Is there something you need to tell me?"

Not knowing what she's found, I turn around

just as she's pulling one of Mum's old dresses from a box. It was the one she's wearing in all of my fondest memories, hence why it's in here sitting in a box.

"I know you're into all kinds of shit, but I didn't have dressing up as a woman as one of them." She laughs as she goes to refold it but before she has a chance, I snatch it from her hands. I bring it to my nose, but the smell I long for is no longer there. It's just a damp musty smell that doesn't make me feel any better. "Scott?" Her eyes take on that soppy look they do whenever she turns Doe's way and I hate it, but the lump in my throat grows too big for me to be able to tell her to stop it.

Reaching out, she places her hand on my forearm in support.

"It's okay. I... uh... won't tell anyone."

A laugh falls from my lips at the expression on her face.

"I don't dress as a woman, Suki. This was... this was my mum's favourite." Sucking in a deep breath, I finally admit the truth. "Most of this stuff in here belonged to her. I've not been able to part with it."

Her chin drops as her eyes bounce between mine. I hate that I can see the tears swimming within them, but there's not much I can do about it. Thinking of Mum and that time of my life turns me into an emotional mess at the best of times. Standing here, surrounded by her stuff definitely doesn't make it any easier. My hands tremble as I clutch the fabric tighter.

"Sit down," she encourages.

I bend my knees and find I slide down the wall I didn't know I'd stumbled back into.

"It's okay to be sad, Scott." She sits beside me and places her warm palm on my jean covered thigh. Her contact and support feels good. It's a long time since I've felt it. I'm more used to a woman's touch leading to something else these days than I am them giving me a shoulder to cry on.

"I should be over this by now," I admit, feeling embarrassed that it still brings me to my knees all these years on.

"I don't think there are any rules when it comes to losing parents. I can't say I know much about the subject seeing as I don't have any."

"Shit, Suki. I'm so sorry."

"It's fine." She looks away from me as she says it, telling me that it's anything but fine.

"I might have lost my mum but at least I had

nineteen awesome years with her. I should be celebrating that."

"You should celebrate her. I know you've not really told me much about her but I'm sure that's what she'd want.

"I totally fell apart towards the end of it all. I've never forgiven myself for not being there in the lead up to her death."

"But you were there in the end," she says, remembering my previous admission about the day she died.

"Yeah but the months before that I'd been sectioned. She told me Dad was looking after her, giving her the support she needed. Turns out that was bollocks. He'd always been a waste of space and only reappeared when he'd heard she was ill in the hope of her insurance money. Arsehole. He went running back to his other family the second he discovered she'd left everything solely to me."

Suki flinches at the hatred in my tone. "Other family?"

Reaching over one of the boxes, I rummage through until I find what I want. Pulling the picture frame out, I hand it to Suki.

"You've got a brother?"

"Pfft, *half*-brother." My lip curls at just the

thought of him and my dad. Deacon was his first born, his special child. The one who got everything while I was left with Mum who had to work her arse off just to put food on the table and keep me clothed. "This is the only photo of us together. Dad thought it might be fun for us to get to know each other, seeing as we were so close in age. It didn't quite go as planned." I look over at the photograph she's holding. We're stood side by side, clearly as unhappy to be there as each other. We were thirteen, old enough to know what the situation was and how it came to be that there was only six months between us. "My dad was a cheating cunt," I blurt out unintentionally.

"Was?" Suki asks hesitantly.

"Ha, no. Sadly, he's still breathing. Fuck knows where though; I've not seen him for years." I blow out a shaky breath. My sadness over going through Mum's stuff mixing with the anger my dad always manages to bubble up inside me.

Suki turns to me, her eyes soft and kind. Something inside me instantly settles. "I understand how important some of these things must be to you. But if we're going to make enough space to turn this into a room for Doe then you are going to have to get rid of some stuff. But—" she adds when I go to cut her off. "I think there are probably a few ways we could recycle some of your mum's things and make use of them in Doe's room. How many clothes of hers do you have?

A small smile twitches at my lips. She gets this. She's not laughing at me, she doesn't think I'm pathetic for holding on to it all for so long, she just understands. Reaching out, I wrap my hand around hers. Her eyes fly to mine and our contact holds, something crackling between us.

Unable to fight the pull, I lean in, not giving my actions one thought. I'm a breath away from her lips when a whimper comes from the other room.

Fuck.

"I'll go. You... carry on." Suki jumps up and runs from the room, leaving me to bang my head back against the wall in frustration.

CHAPTER TWELVE

Suki

Fuuuuuccccccck.

Fuck. Fuck. Fuck. Fuck. Fuck.

I cuddle a crying Doe, but Scott is only a whisper behind me.

"I know you said you've got it, but I couldn't stay there and not know she's okay," he says softly behind me.

I hand her over to her father. His attention, that moment, having passed; his eyes now full of concern for his daughter.

"I think she's just missing Daddy." I say. "Look, she's already stopped crying."

"How am I going to do this, Suki? How will I work when I have a baby to look after?"

I smile. "Like parents the world over."

"But I've no family to leave her with. She'll have to go to daycare."

"Plenty do."

"I'll have to choose one of those with video access so I can look at her throughout the day."

"Scott." I say sternly. "Calm down. Let's just get through today. Your emotions are running high. We can take Doe into your room with us in her basket and then tonight I think we should share a bottle of wine. I'll let you choose a film for us to watch."

He stares at me like an alien has just landed.

"But, Suki. That could be construed as almost... friendly."

"I can always suggest you grow a pair."

"No, no, no. You offered. Dinner and a movie. I'm sold."

"I did not..."

He pouts.

"For God's sake. I'll order a pizza as well."

WE GO BACK to the spare room and Doe lies contentedly in her basket while we carry on sorting through things. We make a pile of the clothing.

"So what were you thinking with Mum's clothes?"

"I don't know how you feel about it, but I'm quite handy with a sewing machine and I thought I'd cut some squares and make a quilt for her eventual bed and maybe some cushion covers?" He winces when I say about cutting them.

"You could keep maybe one or two of your absolute favourites for her to play dress-up in, but ultimately Scott, you need to let go. Your mum is here." I point to my temple.

He nods. "Yeah, you're right. I'll do that. Can you help me choose two you think she'd like to play dress up with and then I'd be very grateful if you could do the quilt and cushion thing. There's no rush. It's not like she can appreciate them yet. Or, if you don't have time, I can find someone and pay them."

"I can do it. I can start it while I'm here. I just need to collect my sewing machine."

"Suki. I know we wind each other up the

wrong way but thank you. Really. It pains me to say it, but I don't know what I would have done without you."

"Can I have that made up as a poster to put on the wall of InHale?"

"Nope, this message self-destructs in twenty seconds."

I snigger and carry on sorting.

A couple of hours later there's a visible floor desperately in need of a vacuum, and a room that needs dusting. The curtains are down and in the washing machine although Scott seems set on her having the perfect bedroom.

"What would you have wanted, Suki?" he says as I collapse onto the sofa, exhausted.

I immediately tense up. "This isn't about me. It's about Doe."

"God, I've fucked up again. Sorry, Suki. I just thought maybe I could give Doe what you didn't have and it could kind of help you process your own stuff maybe. It was a stupid idea, forget I said it."

My eyes fill with tears. Fuck, I don't cry. I never cry.

"Oh, Jesus. What the hell? I'm sorry, don't cry. Insult me or something. I'm a manslut wanker."

I mumble but it's incoherent.

Scott runs into the kitchen and back and holds out a few sheets of kitchen roll. I wipe my eyes and blow my nose.

"What did you mumble?" he asks.

"I said you were a thoughtful manslut wanker. I'm not a very girly girl and I'd be likely to ask for a black bedroom, but I think if I can choose for Doe, she'd love a unicorn-themed room with all pastel colours: pinks, blues, yellows."

"Unicorn-themed it is." He says. "Right, I'm going to make us a drink. Tea? Coffee?"

"Coffee please."

Doe is back in her bouncer. Once I've had this drink, I need to shower this dust and general grime off myself. God, that room was grim. Scott walks back in handing me a drink and plops down on the sofa next to me but right at the other end, thank goodness.

"So my paternity kit should arrive today. It's posted next day delivery."

"Wow. Big stuff. How long does it take?"

"I've paid extra for results within a day so the quicker I get it back to them the better. But by the end of the week I should have the results, though there's no question really is there?" He looks over at Doe.

"Not to me, but you just never know, do you?" I hedge.

"I can't think about it coming back any other way. She's mine. I'm attached. I'd want to be her father now even if she wasn't mine. Every little smile that you tell me could be wind. Her smell. I'm just addicted. What would my flat be like without her noises in it?"

"I get you." I tell him. "I'll miss her too when I go back home."

For a moment he looks panicked. "Sorry, I know you will have to go home sometime. Perhaps there's a flat in my block, like we could drive out the person next door? Then you'd be able to visit and babysit."

"Oh yeah. At your beck and call while you go out shagging."

"I think those days are behind me, Sooks."

"A) I don't think a complete personality transplant is possible in that short space of time and B) if you call me Sooks again I will throttle you with my bare hands and then your daughter will have no one."

He winks. "She'd have you... Sooks."

ANGEL DEVLIN & TRACY LORRAINE

I put my drink on the coffee table and launch myself, pretending to wrap my hands around his neck. At the last minute I decide to tickle not mock strangle. He wriggles as he tries to get away. "Stop it, stop it." Somehow I've ended on top of him straddling his lap. Well this is extremely awkward.

I look down at him, "Erm."

A loud knock on the door means I can clamber off with the distraction of him needing to answer it. "I bet it's your paternity kit," I say.

He climbs off the sofa but looks at me while scratching his chin. "I'd expect that to be left downstairs with the rest of the mail, but I guess it could need to be signed for."

He walks into the hallway and I sit back on the sofa, until I hear the loud words. "How do you know where I live and how could you just leave the kid like that?"

I rush as fast as my legs will carry me into the hallway.

"Well, aren't you going to invite me in?" Doe's mother asks, with a perfectly drawn brow.

"INVITE YOU IN?" Scott sneers. "The woman who abandoned a baby without a stitch of extra clothing, not even a fucking nappy? Fuck off."

"Now, now, Scott. I'm sure I have information about our daughter that would be helpful to you, so I think a cup of tea would be nice. Yes, indeed."

I can see Scott is about to slam the door in her face, but it's true. The leggy blonde standing in the doorway wearing a camel coloured jumper dress and brown boots does need to explain herself. I step forward.

"Come in. Leave your boots in the hall."

She smiles smugly at Scott who is looking thunderous at me, steps past him, removes her boots and follows me.

"We'll go through to the kitchen."

"Where's my daughter?"

"She's settled. You can see her later, maybe, after we've talked."

Scott follows us in. "You've got five minutes, that's your lot."

"I like her attitude much better. You're the bartender from InHale, right? I was under the impression you two hated each other. Was that just an act?"

"It's none of your business. Now what do you

want?" Scott looks about to pick her up by her clothing and launch her back out of the flat.

"Now, Scott, I don't actually think you should be treating the mother of your child like this. If she's yours of course. Arranged a test yet?"

"I'm going to ask you one last time. What. Do. You. Want?"

"Money," she says as cool as she accepts her cup of tea. "Ten thousand and she's all yours."

"Are you fucking joking?" I yell. "You'd sell your own flesh and blood?"

"She was a mistake." The woman looks at Scott. "A very enjoyable mistake, but a mistake all the same. I thought you'd call me, Scott, when I left you your special delivery but I'm guessing you didn't keep my number. Do you even know my name?"

"Nope. You were just one of many, darlin', and obviously not memorable."

Her face falls slightly at that, but she soon recovers her composure. "Ten thousand and I'll give you full custody."

"I don't know if you've noticed but I already have full custody. You're on camera abandoning your child."

"No, I just handed her to daddy because an

emergency came up." She says smugly. "That's what I'll say, and that you refused to give her back."

"We're fighting you for full custody." My mouth blurts it before my brain engages.

The woman starts laughing. "We?"

"Yes," I announce quick as a flash. "I'm his fiancée. We'll fight you all the way."

Scott almost chokes on fresh air. But it's rattled Doe's mother.

"Let's start again, I haven't even introduced myself." She says. "I'm Morgan Durrant. I used to be a socialite until I fell on some hard times, especially that one." She points at Scott's groin. "Now to keep myself on track I need some financial assistance. You can either pay me a little through child support and I'll keep the brat in a box in my flat, or you can have her, for ten k. It's a bargain really."

"What's her name?" I ask.

Morgan just smiles. "What's it worth, darlin'?" She mimics Scott's voice.

"Five hundred pounds. I can go get it from the cash machine now. I want to know her name, her birth weight, her proper date of birth and where she was born. I want to be able to copy her birth certificate. I presume you have it?"

"How very astute of you. I do. Fine. Five hundred for the name. Seems like a good start." I stand up and Scott steps in my way, his jaw set taut. "No, Suki."

"She deserves it."

Morgan looks surprised. "Well, I didn't expect you to say that, but yes, I guess I do."

"Not you. Your daughter." I spit. "I'll be a couple of minutes. The cashpoint is only around the corner." I grab my bag and dash for the door.

I need to get this money and get to know who Doe really is and the details she needs for life, her date of birth. And then if I need to pretend to be Scott's fiancée to fight this bitch for custody, I will. I'll do anything for that baby, anything.

I'm in so deep, I'm fighting to keep my head above water, especially as I withdraw five hundred pounds from the machine that I can ill afford, but some things are more important.

Doe is more important.

Making my way back into the kitchen, I'm actually surprised that I didn't find Morgan back on the doorstep.

She smiles as I walk in. "At least one of you understands me, anyway."

"I want the birth certificate first."

"And how do I know you'll give me the money?"

"You don't, but then I don't think you're in any position to argue if you want to leave here with the cash. Give me the certificate so I can take a photo of it."

"I've got a scanner." Scott says. I nod.

"Pass him the certificate." I demand.

She laughs. "I did you a copy anyway. Here you go. I'll exchange it for the five hundred." She holds it to Scott who has a quick look, nods, and I give her the money. She hops off the chair. "It's a pleasure doing business with you. When can you have the rest of my money?"

"You're not having any more money, that's it. Get out of my fucking flat and I look forward to seeing you in court." Scott fumes.

"You want to take that risk? I'll drag your name all over the courtroom."

"How are you going to afford it, if you're here scrounging for five hundred quid?" I spit.

"I'll find a way. It's what I do. I'm nothing if not resourceful." She strides towards the doorway.

"Don't you even want to look at her?" I ask.

"No, I have what I came for." She says and with that she opens the door and walks straight out.

Banging the door closed behind her we both run into the room to see Doe. She's fast asleep.

"She looks like an angel." I say.

"Maybe that's because she is one." Scott says. "Her name is Angelique Mirabelle Durrant."

CHAPTER THIRTEEN

Scott

I fall down onto the sofa and drop my head into my hands. My heart is racing and my head is spinning. How could a mother of such a beautiful and incredible baby act like that? Like money is more important than her daughter? I feel sick. My stomach turns over just thinking about how easily she took the cash Suki offered and ran as fast as she could. She didn't even give Doe—or Angel—a second look. My heart shatters for my daughter. I swear to her in that moment that I will do whatever it takes so she doesn't ever know the kind of mother she has. So she doesn't feel the kind of abandonment that's surging through my body on her behalf right now.

Suki's voice pulls me from my turmoil. I thought today had already been traumatic enough with my meltdown earlier; *her* visit really was the icing on the cake.

"Hi, please could I order two large pizzas? One meat feast and one Hawaiian." She rattles off my address before putting her phone back in her pocket and falling down on the sofa beside me.

"It'll be thirty minutes."

I nod. Staring ahead at the blank TV.

"Talk to me, Scott. You're worrying me."

"I..." I trail off not really knowing where to start. "I think my life just flashed before my eyes."

When I turn to look at Suki, her brows are pinched together in confusion.

"I discover I'm a dad, and now suddenly I've got a fiancée too."

A small smile tugs at her lips. I notice for the first time that they're not painted bright red. As I look over the rest of her face, I'm struck with just how beautiful she is without her make-up. I'm starting to wonder how much she was using it to hide behind, just like me with my over-the-top personality. I'm well aware that I put on that persona to stop anyone getting close enough to hurt me. Could Suki and I be more similar than we've ever realised?

"Sorry about that. I panicked. I couldn't have her thinking she'd stand a chance of taking Doe... Angel..." She shakes her head in confusion, her short bobbed hair hitting her face. "I refuse to allow that bitch to take her from us."

"From us?" I ask, but I'm not testing her, I'm genuinely interested in how attached to Doe she's become. How set she seems to be on helping us.

"Shit. From you." She chastises herself before getting up and walking to the kitchen and pulling the fridge open. "You haven't any wine," she complains.

"I usually wine and dine women in restaurants, Sooks. You're the only woman to spend any time here."

She looks over her shoulder at me in surprise, but I can't read the look in her dark eyes.

"I'm... uh... gonna run to the shop. I think we deserve a bottle—or two—after that interaction."

"I can go," I offer.

"No, no, you stay with Doe. She'll need a feed soon. I could really do with some air."

I refrain from pointing out that she only just got back from the cashpoint, in favour of watching her pull her boots and coat on.

The flat feels empty and like there's something missing the second the front door closes behind her and I hate it.

Making the most of the quiet and Doe's nap, I run towards the shower. The dust from that room is coating my skin and I hate it.

I have the quickest shower of my life. I hate not being able to hear Doe but if I don't have a shower when I can then I'll never wash again.

I turn off the shower, grab a towel and rub it over my hair as I step from the room to check on her.

She's still sleeping soundly in her bouncer, but she's put her little thumb into her mouth and she's sucking intently. She's too unbelievably cute and I forget what I'm meant to be doing as I drop down beside her and stare at her little face.

I ignore the click of the front door, but it's not until I glance up at Suki, who's walking in with a few shopping bags in her hand that I realise I'm naked with the towel still in my hand.

I stand but it's too late. Her eyes run down my bare torso until they land on my cock. They stay there for just a second too long, giving me ideas. But then she blinks, her eyes find mine and they narrow to slits.

"Do you ever put clothes on?" she barks, turning her back on me and dumping the bags down on the kitchen counter. Glass clatters. So much for her buying one bottle.

"This is my flat. I can let it all hang loose if I want."

"Yeah, when you're alone. Go and put something on. Neither Doe nor I want to look at that before dinner."

"Fine." I turn to walk to my bedroom but feeling her stare I look back over my shoulder. "Nice arse, right?" Her face turns beetroot-red at being caught.

"I'm going to have a quick shower. Don't eat all the pizza if it gets here before I get out."

"I'll see what I can do."

Suki locks herself in the bathroom. I'm not sure if she wants to keep me out or her inside. The thought alone makes me smile. Am I cracking a little bit of Suki's reinforced armour?

The pizza man buzzes as I'm shoving my feet into a pair of jogging bottoms and I almost fall face first in the hallway as I race to go and answer it. I'm fucking starving; no one is taking that pizza from me.

I've got them up around my waist by the time my hand hits the buzzer to allow the guy up. My stomach growls as I wait for him to appear with two steaming hot boxes.

"Thank you," I say, before taking them to the kitchen and resting them on the side while I get out two glasses and pull one of the bottles of wine from the bag Suki abandoned. I also find a punnet of cherries—random—and a tub of ice cream that I quickly shove in the freezer.

I settle myself down on the sofa with the pizzas temptingly close on the coffee table. My self-restraint is threadbare as I wait for Suki.

The shower turns off and I pray that she's not one of those girls that then spends forever pissing about with exfoliators and fucking face cream.

Thankfully I'm right because not four minutes later, the door cracks open and her light footsteps sound out behind me.

"Oh my god, that smells good." Coming to a stop at the end of the sofa, I look up to find her hair wet and her face still flawless and clear of any make-up. She bends over, I assume to put something in her bag, but all I see is a face full of cleavage.

"You know, I'm an arse man really. But that I can fucking get on board with."

She pauses, looks up at me and then looks down at herself. A growl rumbles up her throat. "Scott, I thought we'd drawn a line," she said referring to me agreeing to turn it down a notch the other night.

"Ah yes, Sooks. But see... things have changed since then."

Her cheeks flame red and I know without doubt she's thinking about our almost kiss earlier in the spare bedroom. I'd also put money on her imagining what could have happened next if we weren't interrupted.

"Scott, that was—"

Ha, knew it! But I cut her off because that's not actually what I meant. "We're engaged now, Sooks. I think it's only fair that I get to check out the goods."

Her fists clench and her lips purse; it's almost as cute as if it were Doe doing it.

"Oh come on. Sit down and eat with me." I reach forward for the top box of pizza that has my mouth watering. I'm not sure what's happened to me but as alluring as Suki is right now in her tight white vest top, I want this pizza more. "You know, this is what most women's fantasies are made of."

"Really, how's that?" She asks, going directly for the glass of wine that's waiting for her.

"Me, in only a pair of joggers. You know you want a piece." I rest back, tensing my abs, making my six pack even more obvious. She fights it, I can feel it, but she's not strong enough and her eyes drop to check me out.

"Meh. I've had better."

I splutter. "I find that really hard to believe."

"Well start believing, baby, because I've got news for you. You ain't all that."

I chuckle but sit back up and open the lid of the box on my lap. "Um... what the utter fuck is this?" I stare down at the pizza like I've just found a dead fucking rat on the top of it.

"Oh that's mine." She reaches out and pulls it from me. If I weren't so horrified by what I just saw then I might make a bigger thing about how she just very lightly grazed my cock.

"And this is why we'll never be real friends. This one had better be free of that shit." I grab the second box and sigh with relief when I only find meat staring back at me. "Only fucking devils put that yellow shit on pizzas."

She laughs at me and makes a show of picking up a piece of disgusting warm pineapple and tossing it in her mouth. She chews and then pokes her tongue out to wipe any stray juice. Instantly the pineapple is forgotten as I stare at its journey, wondering just how soft her touch might be. My cock jerks in my trousers but thankfully with the box on top she'd never know.

"What?" she asks, lines forming on her brow. "Have I got sauce on my face?"

"Oh yeah, just a little." I shouldn't fucking do it. It's wrong on so many levels but fuck it. I reach out and pretend to wipe a bit of nothing from her bottom lip. Her entire body freezes when I make contact with her, her eyes darkening even more than their usual almost black colour.

Our stare holds as I swipe my thumb, air racing across my hand and down my arm from her increased breaths.

"Better eat up. You don't want that thing getting any worse than it already is." I pull away and turn to my pizza as if nothing just happened while Suki's eyes continue to stare into the side of my face. Good, I'm glad she's obviously affected by that because on the inside I'm freaking the fuck out with how badly I want to lay her out right here on this sofa.

Eventually, she turns her attention back to her pizza and the two of us eat in silence. We've not even got the TV on to attempt to break the tension that's surrounded us.

CHAPTER FOURTEEN

Suki

I'm a whirlwind of thoughts and emotions and the last thing I should be doing is drinking wine, but I need to just CALM DOWN. I take a huge swig from my glass and finish my pizza; well, as much as I can eat, while I pretend to watch the television. But really my mind is swirling.

Scott is a manslut.

I don't like Scott.

He's surprising me with being a good dad so far.

The emotions he displayed in the spare room... there's more to him...

That woman is a bitch.

I'm so fucking skint now.

Carl is coming at any minute...

"Fuck."

"What?"

"I forgot. My cousin's coming to look at the spare room. He's going to kill me for not ordering him pizza."

I take half of Scott's pizza and put it with the three pieces I didn't manage.

"Hey, hey, hey, that's my food," he protests.

"Only if I find Carl's already eaten," I declare, closing the box.

"Can't you put him off until tomorrow? It's been one hell of a day."

"Nope. That room needs sorting as soon as possible. Especially if you're going to fight that bitch for custody. You need a solicitor as soon as possible too."

He lifts his own glass up and finishes it off. "It's a shame I can't get completely rat-arsed because my stress levels have maxed out."

"I know." I smile. "Once Carl's gone, we can have some more wine and chat, okay?"

Carl arrives half an hour later. He takes measurements of the room, gives me raised eyebrows and nods towards Scott when he thinks Scott isn't looking, and declines the pizza having called at McDonalds on his way. Scott eats lukewarm pizza while he and Carl discuss plastering walls and fitted wardrobes.

"Can I have a look at the little 'un then while I'm here?" he asks.

"Of course," Scott says and we all walk into the room. I watch as Scott picks up Doe and proudly passes her to Carl. My heart bursts and my ovaries ping. Oh God no. NO. We are not having feelings about hot daddy. I called him a hot daddy. Inside I'm having my own meltdown.

I'm Suki Madden. I'm a sassy, take no bullshit bitch. I am not having some kind of feelings for the whole hot daddy/cute baby combo happening over there. Carl is cooing and Scott is telling him all about mother bitch.

"You find her address and I'll change her locks so she can't get out of her own house. Fucking cow." Carl states. "Anyway, I need to be off, so good luck with everything. I'll be in touch about when I can start. I'll try to move a few things around so you and this little princess are a priority.

Oh, and congrats on the engagement." He winks at me. "Gotta say, I didn't see this one coming. She talks about you a lot, but not with love, mate." With that he laughs at his own joke and leaves.

"You talk about me a lot hey, to your cousin?"

"Like he said, it's not good." I refill both wine glasses as we sit back down. Scott puts Suki down in her bouncer.

"Time for bed soon, little one," he coos. She must listen because her eyes close and within a minute she's asleep.

I go into the kitchen and grab my punnet of cherries.

"That's where pineapple belongs. Alongside fruit, not on a fucking pizza." He complains again.

I take a cherry out of the punnet and eat it.

"Mmmm."

"Fucking hell, Sooks, can you not have an orgasm eating fruit? You'll be tying the stem in a knot next."

I raise a brow and then I wink.

"You cannot do that."

"Watch me." I place the cherry stem in my mouth and wait for it to soften and then I push the stem around until eventually I pull out a knotted stem which I place in the palm of my hand.

"You're killing me, Sooks." He groans. Plonking down at the side of me and reaching for his glass, I note that this time he's so near his thigh is touching mine.

"Have you heard of personal space?"

"There should be no space between man and fiancée." He teases.

I decide to play him at his own game. I lean in closer. His eyes widen as my lips hover near to his.

"I was thinking about what you said, about checking out the goods..." I look up under my lashes at him and bite my lip.

"Yeah?"

"I found yours a bit lacking." I sit back and laugh. But it's short-lived because my glass is snatched from my hand and wine spills on the floor as two wine glasses are clumsily put on the table.

Scott's mouth takes my own, commanding, and taking no prisoners, and fucking hell, the man can kiss.

I shouldn't want to kiss him back. I hate him...

Except I don't think I do any longer. I think I actually want to get to know him...

Oh shit.

I kiss him back as hard as he's kissing me. My tongue slips into his mouth duelling with his. I just can't help myself. Everything has been so unpredictable, why should right now be any different? I'm just completely adrift. I don't know what's happening in my own life right now, or who I am anyway, and here, right now, is a hot, warm body to anchor myself to, even if afterwards I hate him all over again. Right now, I don't. I don't hate him, and I certainly don't hate his kiss. He tastes of red wine and tomato sauce. He smells of men's shower gel. My back is pushed against the sofa cushions as Scott trails a hand through my hair. He breaks the kiss, his lips trailing along my jawbone and down my neck. My skin begins to goose bump as he nips the edge of my earlobe lightly, before kissing and nibbling down, down, down. He pushes my vest top up revealing my bra and then pulls down a cup. My breast is exposed to the cool air and pebbles before he even gets to touch me. Then he captures my nipple in his mouth. It's warm and as he sucks, there's a connection straight to my core, like an electric shock there. I gasp. His eyes flit up to mine and I know he's smiling with satisfaction. He gives my other breast the same attention, palming it, rolling my nipple between his fingers and then capturing it in his mouth. I can feel my panties getting wet. At this point I'm not even focusing on my past with Scott, just right here, right now.

My hand trails down his abdomen, pushing up his t-shirt and I trail my fingertips across his chest, teasing his own nipples. Flattening my hand to his chest, I run it down his tight abdomen, feeling every ridge and muscle. I let my hand move lower and I trail over the front of his joggers, caressing his huge hard-on.

Scott uses one hand to pull down his waistband freeing his cock and I take him in my hand, running my tightened fist down his shaft and back up again. The button at my own waistband is undone and I raise my hips so that my jeans can be lowered. His finger slips under the edge of my panties and teases there, slipping in my wetness.

"Fuck." Scott growls. "Stay there."

He dashes from the room and it gives me a moment to realise where I am. On the sofa, possibly and most probably about to have sex with Scott Sullivan, my enemy. My body doesn't care and it's shut my mind down. I slip my jeans off my legs and pull my vest over my head so that I'm left in my undies only. I reach to the coffee table and drink the rest of my glass of wine as my mouth is so dry.

Then Scott is back, once again completely naked, but this time instead of asking him to dress himself, I luxuriate in the hard planes of his body and the mammoth cock that's coming to satisfy my every need.

He positions himself above me, taking my mouth with his once more. Those deft fingers of his slip back under the edge of my panties and he teases, rubs, and then pushes them inside me until I'm gasping into his mouth and pushing back against him.

"So fucking wet. Come for me," he demands.

And I do, I shudder against his body as my core shatters around his fingers, my breath has my chest heaving against his.

He sheathes himself in a condom and then places himself between my legs. Eyes closed, he thrusts inside me and I gasp in satisfaction as he fills me. He thrusts again and pulls back, thrusts and pulls back and I wrap my legs around him, and then he stops. I feel at my face and as I wipe a spot of liquid away, I realise that it's come from Scott's eye.

His brow is furrowed. His eyes filled with pain and regret. "I can't do it. My mind won't let me. I want to, Suki. I want to, so bad."

"Sssh, shhh. It's okay." I tell him. I let him pull out of me and then I move myself. I push him back against the sofa and I remove the condom. On my knees next to the sofa I take him in my hand and I wrap my mouth around his cock. It's a fucking good job I have a good gag reflex. Once again, I let a hand trail up his body, soothing as my fingertips tickle and trail. As he loses himself into my mouth being around him, I firmly grasp him at the base and run my tongue up and down his shaft, twirling around the glans, sucking on him and then begin pumping him slightly as I suck more firmly. His hips begin to rise up to meet my actions and his hand carefully grasps the back of my head. I feel his balls tighten and then he comes in my mouth, pumping into me and then coming down with a couple of extra tremors. He strokes through my hair as I carefully let him go.

"I'm so sorry." He says and I look at a man I've only seen the slightest glimpse of when he was emptying the spare room earlier.

"There's nothing to be sorry for. I should have anticipated that really. It's hardly surprising in the circumstances." I stand up. "Now while I get dressed, why don't you get Doe's bottle ready and let's get her in bed?"

He nods and then he looks back at me again. "Suki. Don't sleep on the sofa tonight. Please. I want you to sleep in my bed. With me. I need you."

And I nod, because right now I don't feel like I can refuse this version of Scott anything.

Cleaning myself up in the bathroom, I brush my teeth and slip into some soft pyjamas. I might be willing to share but I'm not willing to sleep naked. Things are already confusing. We've wandered into unchartered territory and I have no idea where we go from here. Because I know one version of Scott and that's the one that runs a mile after sleeping with a woman. But although we didn't technically fuck, this man wants me to share his bed. I busy myself washing up until Doe is in her cot and Scott is standing in the kitchen doorway.

"Are you ready for bed?"

Turning around, I pick up the towel to dry my hands on, nod and then follow him to his bedroom. He climbs under the covers dressed in pj bottoms but with his chest bare. Hesitantly, I crawl in at the side of him. He doesn't hesitate though. He pulls me towards him into his arms and tucks me into his body.

"You fit there perfectly," he whispers. "I don't

know what the fuck is happening, Sooks, but I'm going with it."

Well, at least I know he's as confused as I am, I think, as my eyes close and I fall asleep feeling happier than I have in a long, long time, while refusing to think beyond the moment. We're up at various points in the night as Doe stirs but then we get right back into bed and into position until light breaks through the curtains and the reality of legal action and paternity suits dawns.

CHAPTER FIFTEEN

Scott

What the hell is wrong with me? I was inside her. Her tight, hot little pussy was rippling around me and the only thing I could think about was accidently getting her pregnant. I put the condom on. I knew it was in date and hadn't been tampered with, but still this little voice in the back of my head was screaming at me. *If it's happened once then it can happen again,* and where would that leave me? Leave us?

Something was changing. The tension between us growing and my need for her following right along with it, but the risk was too high. Doe's only just two months old looking at the date on her birth certificate. She really doesn't need a sibling by another mother because her dad fucked up again.

Jesus, I'm such a fuck up. No wonder my dad focused all his efforts on my *brother*. He probably already knew they would be wasted on me.

My muscles tighten at the thought and I squeeze Suki that little bit tighter. No one's ever been able to calm me down with just a look and a simple touch, but earlier that's exactly what she did. She made the fog lift that had descended over me as I dove headfirst into my past.

She's sleeping soundly next to me and I can't deny it's equally as weird as fuck as it is incredible. A woman has never slept in my bed before. Hell, a woman's never even been in this flat before, well aside from Sarah, Leah, and my aunt, but they don't count. I'd have thought the idea of sleeping beside another person would freak me out, but as it turns out, it's really quite nice. Comforting.

I snuggle closer, drop my nose to her hair and breathe her in.

"Did you just sniff me?" A soft whisper rings out and my entire body tenses. *Fuck.*

"I... uh..." She uses the time it takes me to

hesitate to turn over.

With her head resting on her pillow, she looks up at me with sleepy eyes and mussed up hair. I'm pretty sure she's never looked so breath-taking.

What the fuck is wrong with me right now?

Unable to stop myself, I reach forward and brush a stray lock of hair from her cheek and tuck it behind her ears. Her eyes shutter a little at my contact and my cock only hardens.

"Scott?"

The image of her on her knees in front of me last night fills my mind along with the guilt of not being able to do the job properly. I'm still not sure if I'm not just completely broken in that department but I try not to dwell on it as I disappear under the covers.

"Scott, what the hell are you doing?" She whisper-shouts, obviously trying not to wake Doe. Her fingers find my hair and she grips painfully. Lifting the covers, she looks down her body at me where I'm settling myself between her legs for my mission. "Scott?"

"Don't tell me you don't want it?"

Her eyes darken and the heaving of her chest makes her tits rise, catching my eye.

"We shouldn't be—"

"When did you ever get the idea I followed any rules, Sooks?"

"Never, but—"

"Just let me. I feel like I owe it to you after last night."

"Scott, you don't owe me anything. Actually, that's not true, you owe me at least five hundred pounds, but—" her words falter as I wrap my fingers around the fabric at her waist and pull her pyjama bottoms and knickers down her thighs. "Like I was saying... you don't owe me ahhh... neee... thiiing."

I part her and lick up the length of her and her words turn into squeals of pleasure and my chest swells with the knowledge that I'm not totally broken.

Zeroing on her clit, I tease around her entrance as her hips lift from the mattress trying to find more. And to think she tried to make out like she didn't want it.

I lick and suck at her, revelling in the sweet taste that is purely Suki and push out any thoughts about my failed fucking attempt last night and the fact I swore about a million times in the past that I'd never touch this girl, let alone willingly shove my face between her legs.

"Oh my god," comes from above me. "Don't fucking stop," she demands when she realises I've slowed my movements in amusement. Her fingers tighten in my hair and I get back to work before she pulls a patch out.

With two fingers deep inside her, I find her g-spot and push her over the edge. She screams into the pillow as she's hit with wave after wave of pleasure that has her clamping down on my fingers so hard it sends my head a little fuzzy considering how that might feel on my cock. It's like steel between my legs and my need to plunge balls deep inside her is so fucking strong, but I can't, not after last night. I refuse to put myself in a position to have another freak out. Plus, that's not what this morning was about; it was an apology for not being able to do it properly last night, not foreplay for what's to come next.

I'm just crawling back up when Doe starts to stir. Right on time, baby girl.

"You stay there. I'll go." I climb over to my side of the bed, find a clean pair of boxers from my drawer and pull them on. They do little to hide my raging hard on, but there's little I can do about that.

The second I turn back toward her, her eyes drop to it and her lips part.

"You want a coffee?"

By the time she's managed to remove her eyes from my crotch she finds an amused smirk playing on my lips.

She licks her lips, then glances away from me. "Y- yes please."

After a quick trip to the bathroom, I scoop Doe up from her cot and take her to the kitchen with me to give Suki some space. She's got an early shift today so she'll need to get ready soon.

I turn to take her coffee when it's ready, but I find her in the doorway to the bedroom already dressed and ready to leave.

"Don't you... uh... want breakfast?" I've no idea why those words fall from my lips. I never have breakfast before an early shift knowing that I'll be able to snag something much better from work. I know for a fact that Suki does the exact same thing.

"No, I don't think that's a very good idea. Do you?"

I look into her concerned eyes and start to panic. Have I ruined everything? "Is... uh... this about last night, and this morning?" My hand comes up to the back of my neck as I wait for her response. The churning of my stomach and my racing heart points to the fact that I'm more worried about what she's going to say next than I want to admit. This is why I don't do fucking sleepovers. Although, I must admit it's more because I'm worried the woman will get attached, not the other way around.

No, no, no. That's not what's happening here. I'm just craving a proper sex session.

"Yes. No. Yes. None of that should have happened, Scott. I'm not here to be your plaything. I was here to help with Doe."

Turning, she pulls her bag up onto her shoulder and takes a step forward, ignoring her coffee that I'm still holding.

"I'll see you soon." With that, she kisses Doe on her head and leaves the flat in a rush.

Two things about what she said ring out in my mind. *I was here to help with Doe,* and *I'll see you soon.* Not I'll see you later, or I'll be back after work. No, just I *was* here.

Putting her coffee down, I walk over to the sofa and fall down, dropping my face into my hand. I really did royally fuck this up.

Doe stirs and I've no choice but to pull myself together for her sake.

I feed her, change her, and manage to have a shower with her sitting in her bouncer beside the bath. Suki's scent still surrounds me and as much as I like it, I need to get her out of my head. It seems she's buried her way in too deep already.

It's not until we stop that I realise with all the excitement that happened yesterday that I didn't receive the DNA test I'd ordered on next day delivery. I'm just pulling up my confirmation email when the buzzer goes off.

I'm ready to give the delivery man a piece of my mind for it being late when a soft female voice comes through the speaker.

"Hey, it's Sarah. Oh and a delivery man for you. Can we come up?"

"Yes," I say eagerly, much to her amusement and I unlock the front door.

I secure Doe in her bouncer and go to the door.

"Hey, come in," I say to Sarah, moving aside so she can enter. She does as she's told, and I don't need to look behind me to know that she's gone straight for Doe. She's a total baby addict.

"This was meant to come yesterday."

"I'm sorry, sir. There was a mix up at the depot."

"Not good enough. I paid for this to come yesterday."

"I understand that. There's a number on this card that you can call to complain."

"Fantastic," I mutter with a roll of my eyes, signing his little PDA and letting him run away.

"I'm pretty sure she is hands down the best thing you've ever done in your life." Sarah calls out.

I find her, as expected, cradling Doe to her and staring down mesmerised into her big brown eyes.

"I can't help but agree. Coffee?"

"Always."

"Do you want to feed her?" She looks up at me with an 'are you fucking kidding me' face and I laugh. "Okay then. Where are your sprogs?"

"With their grandmother. I've got a few hours to myself, so I thought I'd come make sure you're okay and drop that off." She nods over to a pile of bags I didn't notice her carrying when she came in.

"So, you look like you're handling this, but I know you, Scott. This can't have been an easy transition for you."

"I don't know what I'd have done without

Suki's help." Just saying her name causes an ache in my chest that I really don't like.

"Oh wow," Sarah says, staring at me with wide eyes.

"What?" I ask sceptically.

"That look. Those soft eyes, that soppy smile. You've fallen for her, haven't you?"

My spine straightens. "Don't be so ridiculous. I can't stand her."

She laughs. Actually laughs. "Right. You keep telling yourself that. Feel free to tell me that I was right whenever you figure it out."

I narrow my eyes at her. "You know. I might just spit in this." I look down at her coffee and back to her.

"You wouldn't."

"Try me."

Sarah stays for a couple of hours and helps Doe and I do our DNA samples before I follow her from the building to send the pre-addressed box back to the laboratory for testing.

"You need anything, you ring me. Especially if you indeed have fucked it up and she stubbornly doesn't come back."

"She'll come back," I say light-heartedly, but I

don't feel it. "I allowed her to see heaven, there's no way she'll not come back for more."

Sarah raises her brow. She sees through my bullshit just as much as Suki does and she knows this is bothering me more than I'm letting on.

"I'll call Reese later and give her your number, hopefully she'll have some advice for you once you get the results back." Reese is Sarah's best friend and before having her own kid she was a family lawyer. She's talked about her before, but I paid little attention. Now though, I'm all ears for someone who could help me with Doe.

"Goodbye, gorgeous girl. I'll see you soon. I might even bring some playmates with me."

"Isn't she a little young for that?"

"Never, she'll love watching them play."

We say our goodbyes and Doe and I spend the rest of the day together. I want to say it's getting easier, but by the time Suki's shift is coming to an end, I'm exhausted. I'm ready for someone to talk to and for someone to help me a little.

I bathe Doe so she's already in her pyjamas and smelling all cute, but as I suspected, Suki never shows.

CHAPTER SIXTEEN

Suki

I had to get away. It's all too much, so I escaped. Firstly, I went to work where I managed to get through a million (well probably two) questions about Scott and Doe and then I went home. Which is where I am now. In my own flat, with the heating on, in my pyjamas, a big comfy throw wrapped around me, and a large bottle of wine all to myself. Because I need to think, and I need alcohol. The two aren't necessarily the best combination but it is what it is. I also have a punnet of cherries.

What the actual fuck is happening? A few days ago, my life consisted of seeing Carl occasionally, working at InHale and hating on Scott while enjoying my job, and my home routines: shopping, reading, cooking. Nothing too amazing, but regular. I don't really have friends. I've never wanted to talk about my past. Dating is something I do occasionally, again, not really wanting to get into my past has put me off. Now, I've become involved in a two-month-old baby's life, become involved in her father's life and started to develop some kind of feelings for him.

Stockholm syndrome. That's what it must be. Where you fall for your captor. I know he's not exactly kidnapped me, but I've been forced into close proximity with him. That'll be it. So, if I stay by myself for at least tonight and maybe forever then I'll realise he's still a twat won't I, and I'll recover.

If nothing else, it's made me realise that I can't stay how I am. I've not been living my life; I've been avoiding it. Spending time with Doe has shown me that I want a family and if I want that, then I'm going to have to come to terms with my background and put myself out there.

I pick up my phone and skim through the many varied photos I've snapped of Doe. I have no baby photos of myself. No one took any. The first photos I have are school photos that various foster parents purchased. As I left the house, I took them with me, but I left behind any of me and the families. For various reasons they didn't keep me. Sometimes they treated their own kids far better, sometimes it was clearly for the money and they didn't give a shit about me. One lovely couple had to end my placement when the wife got ill. Photos would hurt me. It was better to stick to the occasional school pic and forget everything else.

I wonder what's Scott's family is like? He has a half-brother. He obviously doesn't have anything to do with him. Looks like he had a fabulous mum and a strained relationship with his father.

I take a slug of wine straight from the bottle and flop back against my propped-up sofa cushions. Though I'm missing Doe, it is so damn nice to be in the total quiet. My brain needs space. Scott has to find out his DNA results and he has to sort out what he's doing about Doe's mother. It's not actually anything to do with me. I've spent all that money on baby stuff and then given her five hundred pounds to fuck off. Far too involved. I scold myself. You've lost your head thinking about this baby. Thinking about your past.

It's time to leave Scott to get on with it and get back to living my own life. It'll be hard but I need to distance myself from Doe. She's not mine. She's the daughter of a colleague... and even that's not confirmed. What I need to do is to get my belongings from Scott's, ask for my five hundred pounds back, and then concentrate on my own life. Perhaps I could go speed dating or let Carl set me up with someone?

Stretching out on the sofa, I pull the blanket around me and immerse myself in wine and the television.

My phone pings with a text message. I'd told myself to turn it off and yet, part of me, the part I'm unwilling to face, made me leave it on. I reach to the floor and swipe the screen.

Scott: Where are you?

Do I want to start a conversation with him? I sigh but start typing.

Suki: Home on the sofa.

Scott: You could have said you weren't coming back here.

Suki: I kind of did.

Scott: Doe misses you.

Suki: No she doesn't. She's totally unaware of what's around her. Don't do that to me.

Scott: I'm sorry, about us well, 'doing bits' like they say on Love Island. If that's what's keeping you away, we can try to go back to being in a truce of just not hating each other.

Suki: I stayed a couple of days while you got more used to parenthood. I'm sure you've got this now. I have my own life. A life I need to get back to living.

Scott: Okay. Well, I guess there's not

**really anything else left to say. Enjoy
your night.**

And that's it. There are no more messages. I
drink another heap of wine until I eventually drag
myself into bed and more or less pass out.

THE NEXT MORNING, I wake with a headache
and thank God it's my other day off this week. Carl
texts me to say he's spending the day at Scott's
house plastering the wall that needed it and doing
the storage. It's only one day's work, so once the
plaster is dry, Scott will be able to get the room
ready for Doe. I guess at some point he'll start
calling her by her actual name? Maybe he already
has? I feel a pang in my heart at not seeing her. It's
been almost twenty-four hours now.

She's not yours, Sooks.

Fuck, I'm calling myself his nickname for
me now.

I realise that it's not just Doe I'm missing.

After getting ready and drinking two cups of

coffee and eating some toast, I decide to get it over with and go to Scott's to pick up my things and talk to him to clear the air about what happened between us. We were obviously just searching for some comfort. I can say hi to Carl too and knowing that he'll be there in the spare room means a safety net while I talk to Scott; like we can't end up in bed!

So I'm a little surprised when it's Carl who lets me in.

"Oh, hey." I say looking past him.

"If you're looking for Scott and the baby, they're out."

"Oh, where'd they go?"

"I think he's got a date."

My mouth drops open. "What?"

"I overheard him on the phone. Said something about double trouble and laughed. That he'd see her at twelve. Checked she was fine with him bringing the baby."

"Well that could have been anyone. Anyway, you leaving me outside or letting me in?" He steps aside and I walk towards the living room, seeing all Doe's things, all empty and abandoned and it hits me that if she goes back to her mum, this is what Scott would be left with.

"He said he was sure he'd have ruined her for all other men."

"Oh." I sit down on the sofa and sigh.

"What's going on, Suki?" Carl goes out, returning with a clean sheet that he places on the sofa before sitting down at the side of me.

"I don't know if I hate Scott anymore."

"And that's a problem why?"

I pull a face at him. "Because he's Scott the Slut. He's horrendous. Loving and leaving and breaking hearts everywhere. We don't get on. At all."

"But now you've seen he doesn't abandon all women. Because he's committed himself to Doe."

I let out another large exhale. "Yes, and also, he shared a little of his past. I think he's messed up like me, Carl. I don't know for definite, but I just got the impression that there's more under the surface."

"So get to know him some more. Make an informed choice. If you're interested that is."

"Don't you think I'm an idiot? This is the guy I've moaned to you about for so long."

"People can change, Suki. He's had a major life event that's hit him for six. Maybe he'll return to his twat bastard ways, maybe he won't. You have to decide whether you're interested in getting to know him or not, or whether your interest is just in the baby, given it has reminded you of your own past."

"Christ, I have lots to think about. Anyway, sorry, I'm keeping you from your work. I'll just get my things and then I'll get out of your hair."

"Get your things?"

"Yeah, I need to go home. Scott needs to learn to take care of himself and if he is out with a woman, well it looks like he's already getting sorted. Bit irresponsible if you ask me, especially if he's going to have a custody fight on his hands, but not my problem."

Carl folds his arms across his chest.

"Uh oh, lecture coming."

"Suki. You need to talk to him. If he's going to do something to jeopardise his care of that baby, you need to point that out. Think of Doe, not Scott. And if you are taking your things and going, don't do it behind his back. If he let you stay here, someone he considered a mortal enemy, then not being funny, but the guy can't have many friends, or family for that matter."

I think about his half-brother. "Okay. What about I stay and help you with the room? I can be your assistant. Then I'll be here to talk to Scott when he gets back."

"Sounds like a plan. And your first job is to put the kettle on."

I roll my eyes at him but make my way into the kitchen. While I wait for the kettle to boil, I decide there has to be a logical explanation. Carl heard him say some things, but I know from the other night that Scott isn't willing to stick his dick anywhere just yet. Unless his problem was specifically with me, and he doesn't mind creating kids the world over as long as I'm not the mother of them.

Deciding I've spent enough time in my head, I go and throw myself into helping Carl. After all it's Doe's future room, it needs to be the best it can be.

By the time the room is done, I've had many hours to think and I've decided that I am definitely going to sit and talk to Scott. Explain that we've complicated things by ending up in bed. That we need to have some space where he can work out things with his daughter and his ex. Then perhaps if he does feel something for me too, we could just get to know each other slowly. I scrub a hand through my hair. God, even in my head it sounds pathetic. I've just started to become another one of his desperate harem. They say there's a fine line between love and hate. It was so much simpler when I couldn't stand the man.

Carl goes home and I decide to do some housework next. Nothing major, just a bit of tidying. I go into the kitchen to put a bit of laundry on. While I'm in the kitchen I hear the door going and then there's a ton of laughter. I walk out into the hall.

A woman with long dark hair and pale-blue eyes walks in wearing just a bra. Behind her is Scott who is creased with laughter and behind that is another woman who is also laughing though fully dressed. I can see the pram behind the dressed woman.

"Oh my fucking God, Scott. You brought two women home when you're supposed to be looking after your daughter? So that's what you meant by double trouble; you're having a fucking threesome. Why did I think you had a decent bone in your body?" I yell. "I've a good mind to take Doe with me, but unfortunately she's not mine. The poor cow stuck with you and her waste of space mother. Make sure to put her down safely before you start fucking, won't you?"

The women are looking at me stunned.

Scott reaches out for me, but I smack his hand away from me.

Well at least now I know. Once a player, always a player, and now I'm one of the fools who thought he could be different.

CHAPTER SEVENTEEN

Scott

Sarah phoned to say that Reese had agreed to meet me later that afternoon. I must have sounded a little frantic on the phone because she immediately offered her assistance. Doe's been grumpy all morning. I've done everything I'm meant to. I've given her the colic medicine exactly as per the instructions, but nothing I do seems to make her happy this morning and I hate it. The only thing I can put it down to is her missing Suki. That's the only thing that's different.

Sarah suggests getting some air and says she'll

meet me with her brood. Hopefully that'll cheer Doe up.

We'd not even made it to the park and Doe had fallen asleep. I sit on a bench with her while Sarah tears around the park after the twins. It looks exhausting.

Eventually they don't even notice when she walks over to me and falls down onto the bench.

"Kids keep you young, that's for sure."

"We are young," I point out.

"Depends on who you ask," she says with a laugh. "So what's got that permanent scowl on your face? It can't be this little angel, she's sleeping so peacefully." Hearing Doe's real name is a pang to the chest. I really should start calling her it, but every time I open my mouth to do so, it gets stuck on my tongue. *She* gave her that name, the woman who wants to exchange her for cash.

"Suki didn't come back," I blurt.

"Why? What did you do?"

I shrug, not all that happy that she assumes it's my fault. "Nothing new. I think she's freaking out about what happened between us."

"Can't say I blame her. She's probably sworn time and time again not to touch you and yet she caved to your manwhore ways anyway."

"It wasn't like that," I admit. "It wasn't just a hook-up. It was... it was—"

"More?"

With a sigh, I go for honesty. "Yeah."

"You just need to talk to her, Scott. Man up and tell her how you really feel."

"I don't know how I feel."

"Okay. Do you still hate her?"

"No."

"Do you think about her all the time?"

"Yeah."

"We already know you want to screw her, that's a given knowing your rep—"

"We haven't actually... fucked."

"Oh?"

I drop my head into my hands and say as fast as I can that I couldn't do it.

"Jesus, she really has got you all messed up." Sarah's hand lands on my back and she rubs gently as I sit in silence.

"My advice still stands. Just talk to her. You might find that she's as confused as you are."

Silence falls around us as we watch the twins play.

"Right, come on. Emmett should be home by now so we can drop off the monsters."

We take the short walk back to Sarah and Emmett's home before jumping in an Uber and heading towards the cafe where we're meeting Reese.

Sarah's talked about Reese briefly a few times so it's not hard to pick her out of the customers when we walk in. She's dressed in a sharp navy suit, her hair is perfectly smooth and her make-up is flawless. She's kind of scary and probably not a woman I'd have approached on a night out for fear she'd claw my eyes out if I propositioned her.

"Reese, this is Scott." Reese looks up and runs her eyes down my body as she judges me. I can almost read the words, 'manwhore, check,' in her eyes. "Scott, this is Reese. I'll go and get drinks. What would you like?"

"Flat white and a bottle warmer?" I ask thinking that Doe's probably going to scream the place down soon.

"Sure thing. I'll leave you to get acquainted."

"I...uh..." I fight for the right words under Reese's intense stare. "I really appreciate your help."

"It's no problem. I used to live for this. We've met before. Kind of. I've eaten at InHale. Watched you and that bartender in action."

I unstrap Doe from her car seat and pull her into my arms. I change the subject from Suki.

"What changed? How come you're not still in law?"

"My own version of what you've got right there. She's gorgeous." Her eyes turn soft as she focuses on Doe and I see a totally different side to the woman at the other side of the table. "So Sarah's given me the basics, but let's just start from the beginning so I don't miss anything."

I begin with Doe's mum turning up at the restaurant on Saturday before Sarah joins us and sets about digging through Doe's nappy bag for her bottle so she can prepare it while I talk.

Talking to Reese is incredible. Hearing actual solid legal advice, not just someone's opinion gives me real hope for Doe's future.

"We obviously need those DNA results. If those come back negative, then this is going to turn into something much bigger."

"They won't be negative," I state, one hundred percent sure that Doe is my baby.

"Okay. I'd also like to see your flat, if possible. It'll be important that should you be granted custody that you have a good home. I'll help you build the best possible case that will give you every chance of getting custody, but you've got to do what I say."

No sweat there, this woman's scary as fuck, If she told me to jump I'd immediately ask how high. The last thing I want to experience is her anger. I shudder at the thought.

Doe screams bloody murder the second Sarah tries to put her into her car seat. "It's okay, I can carry her if you two want to keep talking."

I push Doe's empty pushchair as we begin the short, but cold, walk back. I know I've got Carl there working on Doe's nursery and I can only hope that proves to Reese just how serious I am about getting custody.

Doe continues crying on Sarah's shoulder as we walk but it's not until we're inside my building that we learn what the issue is.

"What's up baby gi—ah."

Reese and I turn just in time to find Sarah holding Doe out in front of her while she pukes right down her front.

"I said I'd help look after her not get covered in your daughters sick," she moans, passing Doe to Reese and looking down at herself with a 'what the fuck do I do now' expression on her face.

"Oh come on, this is your job. It must have happened more times than you can count."

"Not the point," she snaps before shocking the life out of me. She reaches behind her and pulls her jumper from over her head leaving her standing in just a lace bra.

"What? Don't even try to look shocked. You've seen them before."

"Yeah, like a million years ago."

Doe coos at Reese as she places her into her seat, probably not wanting to get sick on her fancy suit. "Looks like we found the issue."

We're still laughing about the whole thing as I push the key into the lock and open the front door. I allow Sarah to go first, intending to go straight to my room to find her a shirt to wear but we come up short when we find a short feisty woman staring at the three of us with her hands on her hips and her lips pressed into a thin line.

She shouts something about threesomes and taking Doe, her words getting louder and screechier with each one that passes her lips.

The three of us stare at her in utter disbelief. Once she's run out of steam, Sarah turns to me and whispers in my ear. "She's jealous as fuck right now. You are getting that right?"

The thought that she might be right warms me from the inside out. Could Suki be feeling things for me like I am for her?

"Sooks." She fumes and I can't help but laugh. "This is my friend Sarah, and her friend Reese who's a family solicitor. I met with her to get advice about getting custody of Doe."

A slow breath leaves her, her shoulders sagging and her chest deflating as my words settle in her head.

"So... so why is she...?"

Sarah sees where this is going and holds her sticky jumper in Suki's direction. "Doe just barfed all over me. I wasn't sure what else to do to stop it dripping down my jeans."

Suki's lips curl up as if she's imagining it before she nods. "I've got some clothes here. Would you like to borrow something?"

"That would be awesome, if you don't mind."

Sarah follows Suki over to the sofa where I now see her packed bags are. My heart drops. She really is going home.

"Thank you," Sarah says before turning to Reese. "Have you seen enough?"

"Uh... yeah, I think so."

I want to laugh because Reese is barely inside

the flat, but she agrees and pushes Doe farther into the flat. Suki's eyes immediately fall to her and a smile forms on her lips and she rushes towards her. It's nice to know that she missed one of us at least.

"I think it's best we leave you two to it," Sarah whispers. "Don't let her out of this flat until you've told her how you feel. And by tell her, I don't mean show her."

After saying goodbye to Doe, I thank Reese for all her advice and help and they both see themselves out. Suki and I both stay exactly where we are, our eyes locked as she slowly rubs Doe's back.

"I... um... I'm sorry?" It comes out as a question and I can't help but laugh. Even when she's in the wrong she doesn't like backing down.

Walking over, I take Doe from her arms and place her into her bouncer. Thankfully she's happy now she's covered Sarah in puke. By some miracle it seems she managed to not even get a splash on herself.

I stand to full height in front of Suki before taking her cheeks in my hands. She flinches at my contact but she soon relaxes into it.

"I missed you," I whisper, staring deep into her eyes before leaning down toward her lips. Her head tilts. It's barely visible but it's enough for me to know that she's in. Sarah's warning about telling her, not showing her, sounds out in my head and I tell myself that I will right after I've— I'm too slow, Suki reaches up on her tiptoes and crashes her lips to mine. I stumble back a little in surprise before lifting her into my arms. Her legs automatically wrap around my waist and I lower her to the sofa, covering her with my body and giving her everything I have, well... the PG version seeing as we have a young pair of eyes on us.

CHAPTER EIGHTEEN

Suki

After kissing for what feels like forever but is probably only five minutes or so, I push Scott away from me and we sit close together.

"What's happening here, Scott?" I ask and then I wince. "Oh fuck, I've done it. I've become one of them."

"One of who?" Scott's brow furrows.

"Your fan club."

"Suki." He says exasperatedly. "You are not one of them. Can't you see that? They don't come to my house. I don't see them more than once, and I certainly wouldn't let them spend time with my daughter. They don't sleep in my bed, and I don't want to kiss them over and over and over."

"Oh."

"Suki. When I was alone last night I was thinking about when we stopped, you know, when I stopped; and yes, I think it being the first time since Doe-gate happened and being scared of lightning striking twice might have been the case, but I also think that I was scared of what it might mean. Because I know if I fuck you it's not going to be a one-time only deal. I can't believe I'm saying this, but I'm actually starting to like you. A lot."

I sigh in relief. "I'm starting to like you too. This is ridiculous, right? We've detested each other all that time."

"Look, I ragged on you because underneath I knew you were right. I know sleeping with a multitude of women and binning them off isn't anything to be proud of, but it was a life I could cope with. No real drama other than a few stage-five clingers. I think giving you shit was a defence mechanism."

"I just didn't like seeing how you treated women. They have feelings, ones you walked all over. I don't completely know your family history, but I'm guessing the reason you're acting like that and guarding your heart has some part in it?"

"Some, I'm sure, but it's who I am. Well, no, who I was. Before Doe, and before, well, whatever this is. I enjoyed being single and having lots of sex with no ties." He sees me flinch. "If I said otherwise, I'd be lying, Suki. It's this that's different." He motions between us.

"But is this..." I mimic the same motion, "just because of what's happening with Doe?"

"I don't think so." He moves back closer so he's millimetres from my face, "I think this was inevitable."

"Why?"

"Because I loved to hate you. Looked forward to my shifts. Loved watching your face scrunch up when I wound you up. Wondered what you'd look like if I spanked your arse."

My breath hitches.

I think he's going to kiss me again, but instead he sits back against the sofa.

"I knew Sarah from her living next door to my auntie. I stayed with my auntie when my mum got sick."

"And you ended up in hospital."

"Yeah, I couldn't take it. My father was a twat

who messed with my mother's head. My mum was my one constant. I couldn't handle my dad having moved back in. He did it while I was at my aunties because he knew if I'd been there, I'd have thrown him out, teenager or not. Mum fell for it like she always did until she started to get better. Then he was gone again, back to his first wife, Deacon's mother."

"Because he thought she'd die, and she didn't?" I can't believe what I'm hearing.

"Yep. The stress of trying to live with him, knowing what was happening... well, I ended up in hospital, like I said, sectioned. He left and my mum got sick again, fast growing secondaries. I should have been there and I wasn't."

"Scott, it's not your fault you got sick."

"My father didn't want to know. When she died and I told him I was now alone. He said I was nineteen and to get on with it. How does a dad do that? Deacon more-or-less always got my father's attention. He got the college and university education which led to his swanky job, while I floundered and ended up working in a bar."

"And you don't have anything to do with Deacon?"

"Absolutely not, because he's not a nice person. He's too much like our father."

"So you don't see your father now at all?"

"Rarely. He moved on again. Left Deacon behind too. Fuck knows where he is now, but no doubt he's fleecing them." He huffs.

"Huh, wonder what your brother thought of that."

"Who knows? Too busy living life in the fast lane probably. He's a celebrity journalist. Always shagging the hottest new star. He part-owns B.A.D. Magazine. Anyway, I don't want to talk about him anymore."

"Shit, your background's so fucked up, it makes my life look relatively normal."

"You said you were Doe. You were abandoned?"

"Yep. Short version: my mother was fourteen, I was given up. Found out my dad died aged seventeen, but I have an auntie and uncle on that side and their son, Carl, who you now know."

"Fuck, that's grim."

"I didn't have an ideal upbringing, but life's what you make it, isn't it? I get by now."

But the truth is, I don't want to 'get by'. I want

an amazing life. The family life that Doe has made me realise I crave.

"I don't want Doe to become a victim of her beginning. If Morgan gets her back, then what will her future be? I have to fight for her, all the way. I want to be the father that I never had."

My eyes fill with tears at his words, and because I want to be the mother she needs too. But I keep that to myself. It's too early. I'm just some kind of honorary auntie.

I decide to break up the seriousness of everything with distraction. "Well, Carl finished in super quick time because he had an awesome helper. Want to come see Doe's room?" I ask.

"Sounds like a fantastic idea." He gets off the sofa and holds out a hand to me. I accept it and he pulls me to my feet.

He gets Doe from her bouncer. "Let's go see your room, baby girl." He says and I lead the way, opening the door and stepping to the side.

The room is clean and tidy. Inside Scott takes in the newly plastered wall. "You need to keep the window open as much as you can so the plaster can dry." I inform him. Carl assembled a wardrobe and made shelving fit around it on one wall. "Once it's dried you can paint and then we can get all her unicorn things in and she can move in."

"It's going to be perfect. You think so, Doe?" He looks at me. "What am I going to do about her name? I don't want to call her Angelique. That's what the bitch named her."

"So call her Belle, maybe, from her middle name?" I suggest. "She's a princess, right, so why not give her a princess name?" He looks down at his daughter. "What do you think, Belle?" She blinks twice. It's a coincidence and possibly dust in the room getting in her eye, but we laugh and take it as an acknowledgement.

"Hey, Belle." I say. "I'll buy you a whole library if your beast of a Daddy will let me."

That night Belle has an unsettled night, so we nap when we can, taking it in turns and sometimes cuddling up together when we end up in bed at the same time rather than walking around and consoling a miserable Belle.

The next morning, I actually pour myself two separate cups of coffee as I contemplate having to go into work that afternoon.

"I'm dead." I tell Scott, who is also yawning repeatedly while he switches on his laptop.

I see his face seem to go paler.

"What is it?"

"They've emailed the results. They're here. Fuck, I daren't open the attachment. You do it."

He pushes the laptop towards me.

I click in.

"Congrats, Daddy." I repeat the words I said to him that few short days ago back at InHale. "It's a girl."

"Really?"

I nod and turn the screen around so he can see the results for himself. He's crying and I'm crying and then Doe joins in so we're all wailing, but for two of us at least it's tears of joy.

"And now I know that for definite, that cow is never having my daughter. Never," he states. "I'm going to come into InHale with you today. I need to talk to Jenson and update him about what's happening and how I can work around Belle. I can't stay off forever. This is five days already."

"If he's okay we can work it between us if you need to get back to work. I don't mind looking after her in my spare time. It's not like I have anything else to do."

"Suki. I appreciate the offer but that's one hell of a commitment to make to a child that's not yours."

I feel like he just slapped me. It's a stark reminder of my place here. The person he's started to like, and the woman who's helped out for a few days.

"I'll ask Sarah if she knows any reputable childminders, ones who won't hand the kid over to the mother if she shows up." He bites on his lip after saying it. "Fuck, why don't I have money like my fucking brother does? Then I could pay the bitch off and not have to spend my life looking over my shoulder. As it is, I don't even know how I'll pay my court fees. God, this is all such a mess. A complicated mess."

Knowing I'm becoming part of the mess, I decide this is time to excuse myself. "I've a few errands to run, so I'm going to go do them before I start work. I'll catch you there later, okay?"

AS I LEAVE the apartment building and begin walking, someone jostles me from behind. I turn around to see what's happening and come face to face with Morgan, who is rubbing at her nose, her hair dishevelled and her eyes unfocused. She's standing next to a tall, thick set man, who in stark contrast to her looks clean and tidy. I note he also has a Rolex on his wrist.

"I need more money," Morgan slurs in my face, her rancid breath making me wince.

"Well, I don't have any for you. I gave you the maximum I could take out."

"Then I think I'll just go get my daughter back right now," she says, her eyes narrowing.

"Yeah, got a feeling that's not going to happen," I tell her, "unless the court think a junkie mum is better than a hard-working, stable father."

The man's face darkens. "You said you were going to be able to get my money today."

Morgan waves him off. "I will, Tony. I just need to talk to the organ grinder, not the monkey."

"I don't have time for your shit today, Morgan." The guy says. "You owe me at least a monkey by tonight, ideally a grand." He lifts her chin up and stares hard into her eyes. "Sort it." He moves over to me. "You got any sense you'll help her out cos I know where that baby lives now. Gotta be worth a few in ransom."

My heart beats so hard in my chest I feel like I might die. The guy walks away and Morgan goes running after him. I hear her say, "well, can't you take her and sell her or something. There's a market for babies isn't there?"

I turn towards a nearby hedge where I throw up the coffee I drank that morning. What the actual fuck. I need to warn Scott, but what the fuck can we actually do? Call the police, yes, but how do we keep these kinds of people away? I try to call Scott, but his phone says unobtainable. I wonder if his battery has run down. I'll keep trying.

Then I remember what Scott said about his brother. Rich and a total bastard. I begin Googling B.A.D. magazine. I need to speak to him and fast.

CHAPTER NINETEEN

Scott

The second Belle falls back to sleep after her morning bottle, I grab the blanket that Suki had been using on the sofa and curl up under it.

I don't even remember lying down but when my eyes flicker open once again, I'm thankful that I feel a little more alive than I did first thing.

I sit up, looking and listening for Suki when I remember that she's already left. Disappointment floods. How can I go from never wanting a woman in my bed, to wanting to wake up to only one every day, so fast?

With Belle still asleep, I grab a shower and I even manage to have a quick shave before she stirs. She's obviously exhausted from her bad night as well.

I get us both dressed, Belle in the cutest dress she owns and me in my favourite shirt. Something stirs in my stomach. Is that... is that nerves? I only saw Suki this morning, why am I now shitting it about walking into our place of work and seeing her? She's spent most of the last week here. She's seen more of me than anyone has in a long time. Just walking into InHale should be a walk in the park after that.

I decide to walk, seeing as the sun is shining and I'm downright desperate for some exercise. I've not been to the gym since Belle's arrival and my sexercise is seriously lacking, something I hope that can be resolved now Suki and I have confessed that we're both on the same page. I want her so fucking bad after hearing her words to me last night, but I refuse to make my usual mistake. I'm not going to jump in dick first and fuck it all up. Suki deserves more than the way I've treated women in the past. What she said last night wasn't news to me, I was aware that I was an arsehole, taking what I needed and kicking them to the curb as soon as I got it. I knew of what I was doing. I was hiding, protecting myself from having to deal with feelings and heaven forbid... love.

Belle smiles every time she looks at me. There's no escaping that love I was so terrified of before, my chest aches with it every time I look at her, and to have it confirmed in that email, well... it's just everything.

Pulling my phone from my pocket, I pull up my aunt's number. She's been texting for updates but as she told me she would, she's not got involved and left me to it. I'm not sure if she was just going for tough love or if she was worried about the risk of getting attached. It's no secret that my aunt battled fertility for years when she was younger and was never successful. I don't think she'd have coped if she fell in love with Belle and then it turned out I wasn't her dad.

"I've got news," I say before she even gets the chance to say hello.

"Go on."

"She's mine. It's official." I swear I hear her smile.

"Oh my gosh. Are you... are you happy?"

"How are you even asking me that? I'm over the moon. I mean, I knew she was mine the second

I looked at her; but seeing those results, it was like everything in my life fell into place."

"I can't believe you're a dad."

———

"YOU'RE TELLING ME. Can I bring her around to meet you properly soon?"

"Of course. I can't wait for cuddles with my baby niece."

I grin knowing that Mum would be smiling down on us right now. I'm pretty sure she'd have given her right arm to be able to meet her granddaughter, but it wasn't meant to be.

"Okay, I'll be around over the next few days. I'm just on my way to talk to my boss. I need to make some serious changes."

"That you do, my boy. I'm here if you need anything."

"I know, thank you."

InHale comes into view as I turn the corner and after saying goodbye to my aunt, I cross the road, my stomach turning over with anxiety.

Suki's shift's not started yet so Leona is behind the bar. She gives me a double take when she looks up and finds me trying to manoeuvre a pushchair through the entrance. She must have heard the gossip. I can only assume it's been rife here, but she doesn't comment other than to offer her help and rush over. She's got a little one, although a lot older than Belle, so she knows the struggles.

"Oh my god, Scott, she is gorgeous. Look at those cheeks. I just want to squeeze them." Her voice gets all high pitched and squeaky. It's probably because her ovaries are exploding.

"Well what did you expect? She's got my genes." It feels so fucking good to be able to say that with absolute certainty.

"Here's the daddy," Jenson says, emerging from out the back with an amused smile on his face. He looks me over. "Why aren't you covered in puke and looking like the back end of a bus from the sleepless nights?"

"Because she's fucking awesome, plus I had a good teacher." I refrain from explaining that I'm just really good at putting on a show. I might have showered, shaved, and styled my hair, but I'm pretty sure my insides are still sleeping.

"Ah yes. Speaking of which. Where is Suki? You killed her?"

"Ha, funny! She's on a late shift. She'll be here soon."

"Check you out knowing her schedule." Jenson winks at me. He can tease me all he wants; he's not going to see what I'm about to tell him coming.

"Can we have a chat?"

"Sure. Let's go to my office. Everything good here, Leona?"

"Sure is, boss." She heads back behind the bar and continues with whatever she was doing before I arrived.

I follow Jenson through, thanking him when he holds the doors so I can get Belle through.

"So how are things going?" he asks, falling down into his chair.

"Incredible."

"Really?" His eyebrows almost hit his hairline. "I'm not going to lie, Scott. I wasn't sure if you had this in you."

"Thanks for the vote of confidence." I want to be pissed at him, but the truth is that if I'd been warned this was going to happen, then I'm pretty sure I'd have felt the same. "She's mine."

"She is?"

"Yep, so it looks like my life has changed forever and I need to think about how I'm going to manage everything."

"Okay," Jenson agrees, nodding. "Being a

working single parent is hard, Scott. I'm not going to lie to you."

"I'm hoping I might not be single," I blurt, not really expecting to say the words out loud.

"Oh?"

Just as I open my mouth to explain, there's a soft knock at the door and Suki pops her head inside. "Sorry, I don't mean to interrupt but Leona said you were back here and..." she trails off. I narrow my eyes and study her. She looks flustered in a way I'm not used to.

"Are you okay?"

"Oh... uh... yeah, I was just uh... running late."

"Your shift doesn't start for nearly an hour," I point out.

"Oh, right. I know. Do you mind?" She nods to the empty chair beside me and I pull it out for her. I've not got anything to say that she can't be here for, so it doesn't bother me.

"So, you were saying?" Jenson prompts.

I look to Suki and back to him. "I've met someone," I announce. Suki's eyes fly up to me and her body noticeably tenses, but I don't move my stare from Jenson, who looks as shocked as I was expecting. "She's pretty awesome. Feisty. Doesn't take any of my shit, is an incredible mother figure to Belle, and is so fucking supportive of me... when she's not wanting to rip my jugular out, that is." His eyes flick to Suki as he starts to put two and two together. "And I think you know her."

Turning to Suki, I take her hand and lift it to my lips. Her eyes instantly soften and a smile twitches her lips.

"Fuck me, has hell frozen over?"

"I think it might well have because in less than a week, I've become a daddy and I'm pretty sure I'm falling in love."

"Do I need to leave?" Jenson asks with a laugh as we both ignore him in favour of each other.

"No." Ripping my eyes from Suki who looks like she's about to burst into tears any minute, I face my boss. "I need to work, Jenson. I need the money but I'm going to need to cut hours, move hours, fuck knows what, but I really don't want to leave. I love it here and—"

"Just put us on alternate shifts," Suki interrupts.

"Looks like I'm going to have to," he complains. "No one will want to watch you two all loved up. They come here for the banter and bitching." He rolls his eyes and the two of us laugh.

"Oh don't worry. I still hate him."

"Yeah, and she's still a bitch, what can you do?" I shrug and laugh when she slaps my shoulder.

"What have I done?" Jenson complains watching us tease each other. "Right, I'll look at the schedule, but I can't promise it will always be possible, especially during busy periods but I can offer my wife as a babysitter." He winks and I already know I'm going to be taking him up on that offer. "Do you want to cut hours?"

Jenson pulls up the schedule and after a lot of toing and froing we get something that looks kind of manageable before Suki heads out to start her shift.

Jenson stops typing and looks up. "You know, this family thing looks good on you, Scott."

"Thank you. I just hope everything goes in our favour with getting custody."

"If her mum's as bad as you've made out then no judge in their right mind will make you give her back."

"We can only hope." I refrain from telling him about her attempt to sell me my own daughter. "I've got the number of a kick arse solicitor to call."

"I need to check on the kitchen. Use the phone, Scott. Get the ball rolling." He stands from his chair and moves to leave the room.

"Jenson," I call before he leaves. He pauses with his hand on the handle and looks back over his shoulder. "Thank you."

"You're welcome. We're here for whatever you need. All you've got to do is ask."

With a smile playing on my lips, I turn his phone towards me and find the number Reese gave me. Let's get this show on the road.

CHAPTER TWENTY

Suki

I've just started my shift, which I needed to do seeing as Scott is still here. As I see Jenson head into the kitchen, I intercept him.

"Boss, I need a favour." I explain the situation and Jenson's brow creases. "Suki, you need to go and tell him this."

"I will." I try to reassure him. "I did try to call him this morning, but his phone wasn't working and now I've made up my mind to wait. As soon as I've seen Deacon, I will tell him, but not now. Because if I tell Scott now, he'll not let me go."

"I know what he just said about the two of you, but right now, it's his daughter, not the two of yours, and you're going to see his brother. I just don't want you doing anything that could jeopardise what surprisingly looks like the start of a beautiful thing."

"I hear what you're saying. I honestly do; but Scott's out of his depth here with Belle's mother. Seriously. The people she's dealing with and by dealing, I mean 'dealing'. I have to see if I can do something and by the sounds of it, Deacon has money. I'm going to see if he can do anything and that's that. If it saves Doe, I mean Belle, but costs me my relationship with Scott, then that's just how it has to be. Belle comes first."

Jenson sighs. "Okay. How long you gonna be?"

"Two hours tops with travel."

"Okay. Good luck, Suki. I really hope it all works out."

I nod, wait until Scott's left and then I'm out of the door and heading to Canary Wharf.

THE B.A.D. OFFICES are situated overlooking the Thames and the o2 Arena. A stunningly modern, glass-fronted building leads into a sleek, modern entranceway. The ground floor has nothing but a couple of cover photos on the wall of their issues with Kylie Jenner and Taylor Swift, and security guards walking around. Reception is on the first floor. Interesting. You don't even get in the lift until they know who you are.

The reception desk is high white gloss with nothing but a bell visible to the public. A receptionist who looks like she should be gliding down a catwalk smiles at me, showing perfect white teeth. I, in contrast, can barely see over the desk.

"I'm here to see Deacon King." I announce. She stares at me with a little more interest now and I wonder if she's wondering what he could possibly want with me. I Googled him to find out his details. I thought Scott was a prick, but by what I've read, Scott's barely a pinprick at the side of a knitting needle when it comes to the thickness of prickness against his brother.

"You need to go back in the lift to floor five." She hands me a keycard. "Insert this in the lift. It's good for one trip only so don't think to accidentally put it in your handbag."

I smile. "That happen a lot here?"

"Every. Damn. Day. Several times a day."

"Well, not with me it won't, I assure you." She smiles back. I take the keycard and head up to floor five.

Another sleek lobby greets me and yet another reception with yet another model-like specimen behind the desk. I'm asked to take a seat in a lounge which would rival a first class one at an airport. I wonder how much of this business is Deacon's. I know he's a partner in it with four others, my snooping showed me that much, but how much he owns I don't know. I can't help compare this to the life his brother has though.

The receptionist walks over. "Mr King has asked me to escort you to his office. Please follow me."

I stand and brush down my black trousers, comparing my Primark specials at the side of the receptionist's no doubt designer clothing. It's like another world in this place.

The door is pushed open and the receptionist speaks. "Ms Madden is here, Sir. Do you need anything?"

I take my first look at Deacon King. He sits

back in his chair like he's the King of the World. He smiles at me but it's like a snake checking you out before it bites. His smile reveals his perfect white teeth. There's obviously a shit hot dental plan in this place.

"Would you like a drink? Water, a hot beverage, wine?" He drawls.

"No. I'm fine thank you." I tell him and the receptionist.

"That'll be all." He gives one small nod of his head and the woman is gone.

"Take a seat." He gestures to the chair in front of his desk in an elaborate sweeping gesture. "Because I'm fucking intrigued that someone connected with my dear brother has made an appointment to see me. I guess he has no idea, or you wouldn't be sitting here now."

"No, he doesn't." I lift up my chin. If this arsewipe thinks he's going to play Mr Superior with me, he can go fuck himself. "But he will."

"So, on the phone you said it was, 'of the utmost urgency'. He run out of condoms?"

I ignore him, determined to cut to the chase. I'm here for one thing and one thing only. Belle. "He found out he was a father. The mother of the child is blackmailing him. She says she wants ten grand. He doesn't have it and to be honest there's no way she's going to settle for that anyway. She's an addict. Scott doesn't know, but she waited for me this morning. Her dealer was with her. He threatened to kidnap the kid."

I jump when Deacon's fist smashes into the desk. "Did he now?" He grits out.

Deacon's blue eyes are striking against his tanned skin and the blonde hair that threatens to flop into his eyes. He and Scott are such polar opposites in looks, yet I expect both equally as magnetic to the women around them.

"This kid definitely his?"

I explain about the last week's events, about the DNA test results etc. "I know you and Scott don't get along. He's explained the weird family dynamics, but can you help in any way?"

He tilts his head as he stares through me. I feel like I'm being MRI'd. "My brother and I have a few things in common, even if we try to deny it, and one thing is that he's a walking dick, puts it in any woman he meets."

"Did."

That earns me a raised brow. "You think you've changed him?" I get a look of pity.

"I don't think, I know. However, right now I

don't give a fuck about that. I give a fuck about his daughter. You going to help me or sit there like some gangster for another few minutes, because I've things to do?"

He guffaws with laughter. "I see what he sees in you now, Ms Madden. Fiery little thing, aren't you?" His fingertips drum the desk. "Morgan Durrant will be dealt with."

"You'll make her a financial settlement? All legal and drawn up. So she's out of our hair once and for all?"

The next smile I receive wouldn't be out of place on The Joker. "Suki. Morgan Durrant will be dealt with. *Once... and... for... all.*" He quotes my words back at me but enunciates each word. "She'll never darken my brother's door again." His tongue licks around his lip. "That baby is my niece. Whatever my feelings for my brother, I'll protect what's mine."

I feel like I've sold my soul to the devil.

"Are you happy with the arrangement, Ms Madden? Because when Scott finds out his brother wants to see the baby he's going to explode."

"At least he'll have a baby for you to see."

"True." He stands, showing me this meeting is over. "Good luck with my brother, Ms Madden.

Oh, and send him my love. I'm sure he'll appreciate it."

Shaking, and trying not to show it, I walk to the door. As it closes behind me, I manage to nod to the receptionist and get myself out of the building before I head into the nearest pub and ask for a scotch. What the actual fuck? Am I in some kind of TV programme? Who the hell did I just meet?

I seriously hope I haven't just made the biggest mistake of my life. Now I have to go finish my shift and then go back to the flat and face the music.

The scotch warm in my belly, I manage to finish my shift and then I Uber back to Scott's place. When I get there, I'm shocked to find the place in almost darkness and for a moment I panic that they aren't there. Until the man himself appears in the hallway and with a finger over his lips he indicates for me to keep quiet and then grabs my hand and pulls me into the kitchen. The table is set with candles and the smell of something tomato-ey fills the air.

"I'd like to take you on a date, but I had a problem getting a sitter, so I thought I'd mock up my own restaurant here." He says, smiling.

"I see restaurants almost every day, they're

overrated. I'll take this place any day." I take my seat at the table.

"Belle's fast asleep. I swear she knows she's where she should be now. She gets more content every day."

I smile as he spoons pasta onto a plate.

"Is everything okay?" Scott pauses partway through serving.

"No."

He leaves the plate on the countertop and sits across from me. "What's going on?"

"Hear me out, all of it, and then if you want me gone, I'll understand. Okay?"

"What did you do?" He growls.

I tell him about this morning.

"You let me come back here tonight, knowing some bastard threatened to kidnap my daughter?" He yells. "Why the hell didn't you tell me at the restaurant?"

"Because I knew it was too much for us to deal with alone. So... I went to see Deacon."

For a moment Scott is frozen in place and then fury coats his features. "You did what? Are you fucking insane? What did you think he was going to do? We don't get on. He hates me. HATES ME. Did he laugh you out of the building?"

"No, he's going to help."

Scott slips into his own seat, his head in his hands. "Deacon's like my father. I told you this. What are his terms for 'helping', which I presume is giving Morgan a payoff?"

"He wants to see Belle."

Scott laughs, a pathetic laugh that's full of the air of someone who's given up. "And I have no choice if I want my daughter kept safe?"

I shrug. "You can call the police."

"We both know the police can't protect us." Scott stares at the table for a long time. "I need to call my brother." He says.

"Okay."

"And I need you to leave." He looks into my eyes.

"W- what?"

"You went behind my back. Belle is mine, not yours. Who the fuck do you think you are? Someone threatens my kid, I decide on the course of action."

Tears begin to spill from my eyes as I stand up. "They didn't just threaten Belle, Scott. They threatened me too, but don't let that get in the way of you being the fucking dickhead I've always known you are."

I snatch up my bag and run from the room.

Fuck Scott.

Fuck Morgan.

Fuck Deacon.

I just hope Belle knows how much I love her, even if I never get to see her again.

CHAPTER TWENTY-ONE

Scott

The sound of the front door slamming reverberates through the flat. Red hot anger fills my veins. Standing, the chair crashes to the floor and blood races past my ears.

She went to fucking Deacon.

Deacon fucking King is a law unto himself. He's cold. Controlling and so far removed from any kind of idea of family he changed his surname at his first possible opportunity. He's a fucking arsehole. I wouldn't trust him to buy me a pint of milk, let alone go to him when someone threatens someone I love. He doesn't have a loving bone in his fucking body.

A thought hits me. He doesn't do anything out of the goodness of his heart. He'll want something in exchange for this. Probably my soul.

Suki had no right going behind my back and making a deal with the devil. She should have come to me. If her or Belle are being threatened, then I'm the one who needs to deal with it.

The thought of Belle instantly cools the fire raging within and when I break through the haze, I realise she's crying.

"Fuck." Racing towards my room, I scoop her out of her cot and cradle her to my chest. "I'm so sorry, baby girl. So fucking sorry." I've no idea what I'm really apologising for. Being a useless fucking arsehole and playing my part in her being here in the first place. For my total lack of discrimination for who I used to dip my dick in and not choosing better knowing it could have resulted in her. For getting too close to Suki and currently feeling like my heart is shattering in half having watched her walk out of my life.

Fuck. I just allowed one of the two good things in my life to walk out.

My heart races and my hands tremble as I

make a decision and pull Belle's polar bear suit from the dresser. "I'm sorry, Belle. Daddy fucked up again, but we need to go and fix it and I'm going to need your help. Like it or not, we're a team now so you gotta support me just like I always will you. You might think you're the baby with stuff to learn but you're soon going to realise that I have too. And I think my first lesson might be grovelling.

I don't bother with my own coat. I just place Belle to my chest in the complicated carry device I bought and together we head out into the night.

I freaked out. I know that. I heard Deacon's name, what she did, and I flipped. I sent her away just like everyone else in her life has. The final pieces of my heart splinters that I've just become one of them.

I move as fast as I can towards her flat with a baby strapped to my chest. For all I know she called an Uber and is already locked up tight inside. If that's the case, then I don't think I stand much chance of getting to her. I need her to be walking. I need to surprise her and attempt to sweep her off her feet. Somehow. Maybe there's another lesson I need. I can get any woman I desire to fall into bed, but to actually fall for me? That's a whole other ball game right there.

"I hope you're praying, Belle. I know you need her just as much as I do." When I look down, I find she's falling straight back to sleep.

We're almost at her flat. The street is empty and only the glow from the dim streetlights illuminates the long road. I squint, hoping to see her at the other end but with the winter fog descending fast I can just about see the end of the car next to me.

I pick up pace, hoping to whoever might listen that I'll catch her at the last minute.

As a little more of the street comes in to view, movement catches my eye. With my arms around Belle so I don't jostle her too much, I take off running.

"Suki," I call, hoping like fuck it's her and not some random homeless guy. "Suki. Sooks." At that last name, the figure pauses. *I've fucking got her.* "Stay there, Sooks. Please, please," I beg, closing in on her.

I come to an abrupt stop when I get to the stairs leading toward her building. She refuses to look up, preferring to stare down at the ground.

"Suki, please. I'm sorry, I'm so fucking—shit." I climb the stairs and come to a stop in front of her. She turns to me and the sight threatens to buckle my knees. She's crying. Tough nut, bitch extraordinaire, Suki Madden is fucking crying.

My chest threatens to cave in on itself knowing that I did it. I caused this. I sent her away after she admitted to doing something to keep Belle safe. She didn't have to put herself in the lion's den with Deacon, but she did, and I doubt she batted an eyelid.

My cold hands land on her wet cheeks and surprisingly when I step closer, she allows it.

"I'm so fucking sorry. So fucking sorry." I rest my forehead against hers. Her unsteady breathing fills my ears and I break that bit more. "I freaked out. You shouldn't have gone to see him, Suki." She tenses but I don't stop. "Deacon isn't like normal people. He doesn't deal with issues like normal people. I hate that my life forced you there. He could have done anything, requested anything in exchange for–" My words drift off as this thought hits me.

"H- he didn't. He didn't request anything of me. But even if he had, I'd have done it no questions asked if it meant Belle was safe and with you. I'd do anything for you two, Scott. When are you going to realise this?"

"I'm so sorry. I'm, I'm screwed up, Sooks. You need to remember that."

Her own hands lifts and she holds onto the side of my neck. "You are not screwed up, Scott. You're..." She trails off and I raise a brow at her as I wait. "You're pretty incredible and you're a fantastic dad."

"Really?"

"It causes me physical pain to admit it."

I let out a low chuckle. "Do you know what I think about you?" Her head slowly shakes against mine. I slide my fingers into her hair and hold tight, afraid she might bolt again when I say the words. It's not the first time today they've slipped past my lips but right now I mean them more than any other words I've said... ever. "I think I'm in love with you, Sooks."

Another sob breaks free from her throat and her body sags a little.

"Come home with us. Make it your home too. Be with us, always. Make us a family." Her cries get louder, especially with the final word, and she steps into my side and wraps her arms around my waist. I'm desperate to pull her into me properly but we're both aware I've got a sleeping baby hanging from my chest.

She says something into my shirt as her tears soak the fabric.

"What was that?"

"Ithinkimightloveyoutoo."

"I'm sorry, again?" She pulls her face out and her teary eyes stare up at me. They glisten in the soft street lighting and I immediately lose myself in them.

"I- I think I might love you too." I gasp, my heart threatening to thunder out of my chest. But then she does something that has my own tears spilling from my eyes. She drops her hand and gently places it to Belle's head. "I love you too, baby girl."

My lips find hers and I kiss her in the cold on her doorstep for the longest time. I've never really been a fan of kissing, just seeing it as a necessary means to a more pleasurable end, but suddenly I realise that I could kiss this woman for the rest of my life and be happy. Being connected to her like this, feeling my heart racing in my chest, knowing she needs me just as much. It's fucking everything.

"Let's go home," I whisper against her lips and she nods. Reluctantly, I break away from her. "Do you need to go in and get anything?"

"I just need you right now."

"Fucking hell, Sooks. You're killing me."

She drops her hand to the front of my trousers, palming my solid dick. I wasn't actually just referring to my need to bang her into next week, I was talking about my feelings, but knowing I've already confessed enough tonight, I allow her to continue.

"Hmmm, you might want to stop that."

"Oh?"

"The next time I come I expect it to be deep inside you." She bites down on her bottom lip, her eyes bouncing between mine.

"We should probably go then."

I pull her into my side and with my arm securely wrapped around her waist, we begin the walk back.

"Aren't you cold?" she asks when she realises I'm only wearing a t-shirt.

"Fucking freezing."

"Let's go a little faster, hey?"

We're practically running by the time we turn the corner and towards the entrance to my—our—building. I'm not sure if it's the cold or our desire that has us moving so fast but whatever it is, we're equally as impatient as each other to get inside.

I guess by this point I shouldn't be surprised

that Belle wakes up as we climb the stairs and looks up at me with her wide eyes.

"You want feeding, baby girl?" She blinks her response. "You're on her side, aren't you?" I ask, flicking a look to Suki. "You want to help her torture me a little longer for being a dick?"

"You should probably stop swearing in front of her. Her first word will end up being fuck."

"She's two months old. I'm sure it's fine." Suki gives me a 'don't tell me I didn't tell you so' look before taking the keys from my hands and unlocking the door.

What I really want to do is forget about everything and fuck her up against the hallway wall, then on the sofa, and finally we might make it to the bed; but with the eyes staring up at me, I know that's not happening quite yet.

"Why are you staring at the wall?" Suki asks when she realises I've stopped.

"Just making plans."

"That involve the wall?"

"The wall, you, your legs around my waist. My cock deep—"

"Just feed the baby, Scott." She interrupts, "I'm going to use the bathroom."

It feels like she's gone for-fucking-ever. I'm

sitting on the sofa feeding a sleepy Belle when she eventually reappears.

"Fuck, you're beautiful." I can't stop the words falling from my lips. I take her in from head to toe.

She's brushed and fluffed up her hair, her face is clear, and her eyes are much less red after her crying and hungrier for what's to come. I drop my eyes over her jumper and the slogan 'And what?' written across her breasts. I smile at even her clothes having attitude. I continue my journey down, over her skinny jeans, and to her sock-covered feet; they're covered in little hearts showing just a little of her softer side that I've somehow managed to discover.

"She asleep?" she asks, looking at Belle in my arms.

"Pretty much. She keeps waking and having a little more."

Suki turns and grabs her phone from her bag. Seconds later a soft and sexy beat fills the room. "Don't move."

"Okay." I settle myself back a little, anticipation building to see what she's going to do.

"Tell me what you want, Scott," she demands.

"You." The answer is simple and straight to the point.

"I'm going to need a little more detail than that."

"I... uh..." I stutter thinking how I can express that I want everything to this incredibly selfless woman standing before me.

"Whoa, Scott 'The Player' Sullivan. You're not nervous, are you?"

I swallow. "You know what? I think I am." This is new territory for me. I don't just want Suki for the night, I want her for forever, and that's exactly what she's standing there offering. I hope.

She laughs but doesn't move aside from holding her hands out from her body. "So come on, tell me what you need."

CHAPTER TWENTY-TWO

Suki

Scott stands up with Belle in his arms. "I, we, need you, here, all the time. Forever and ever."

I swallow. "You know this has been the craziest period of my life ever, and that includes me being abandoned?"

He sweeps the hair off my ear and leaning down licks at the lobe. "Crazy, but oh so right. Don't you think?"

I think I'm beyond being able to think.

"I'm just going to put Belle in her cot."

He leaves the room and I double check the

playlist I put on. Satisfied, I quickly slip out of my clothes until I'm just left in my bra and panties.

Scott comes back into the room.

"She's already as—"

He comes up behind me. His body warm against my cooling skin. His arms snake around my waist, his fingers trailing up my abdomen.

"What do you want, Scott?" I repeat from earlier.

"I want this undone and off." He says, unclasping my bra and slipping the straps off my shoulder. The fresh air teases at my nipples as the material is removed. He flings my bra away and cups my breast.

Then his hand trails lower and he drops to his knees as his fingers fasten around the waistband of my lacy white panties and he pulls them lower, down my legs, and all the way down to my ankles until I step out of them. I'm now bare to him and he's still fully dressed.

"Take your clothes off." I command.

"Not so fast." He turns me around to face him, clutching at my arse cheeks and pulling me further forward. "You asked what I wanted. I want your legs parted and my tongue between them. I want you riding my mouth hard."

"Lie on the sofa."

He does what I ask, and I sit astride his head and lower myself down onto just above his face. Once again, his hands grab my arse and then his tongue dances in my most intimate place.

"Fuuuucckk." I gasp. "That feels so good."

Scott continues to feast on my pussy. I run a hand through my hair, my eyes closed, as I move above him, becoming more and more desperate to come. He holds me firmly in place as his mouth's motion becomes more fervent and I begin to ride his face, chasing my orgasm. It slams into me and I rock against him riding out the pleasure, my legs turning to jelly.

He flips me until I'm the one lying beneath him.

"Now what do you want?" I ask between breathy moans, my eyes closed.

"I want to be inside you."

I open my eyes. "Scott…"

He places a finger across my lips. "I want to be inside you. To fuck you bare. You're on the pill. I trust you."

My eyes threaten with tears. This man, who's been let down by so many people in his life trusts me.

"I love you." I say.

"I love you too." His mouth drops onto my own and we kiss, a long drawn out kiss full of everything.

When we eventually break off, I raise a brow. "Now do you think you could take your clothes off and fuck me, Scott?"

"No." He says.

"What?" I try to sit up a little, confused at his rejection, and wondering if his fear is back.

"I've fucked many, many women, Suki, and yes, at some point I will fuck you hard, fast, and deep, but right now I'm going to make love to you, and that is something I have never done with another woman, ever."

He removes all of his clothes and settles himself between my thighs. I trail my hands down his body, taking in all the curves and dips of his abs, heading down his happy trail and finally stroking his hard length and guiding him to my entrance. He pushes inside me slowly, and I raise my hips up to meet him. Gently, he fills me to the hilt, emitting soft groans.

"Fuck, you feel heavenly." He states.

He continues to thrust slowly, driving me crazy, as he lowers his mouth in a bruising kiss, his tongue teasing with mine. His finger strokes across my clit and I shiver with his touch.

"Scott, please." I beg.

He quickens his pace and I match his rhythm. I run my fingernails down his back gently, then stroke that fine arse, feeling it flex as he moves inside me.

Then I can feel everything within me build and tighten ready to take me over the edge. I twist my hips up and meet his every thrust until we're frantic, and desperate, and breathless.

He yells out my name as he comes. I feel his cum spurt inside me and then run down my leg. We collapse against each other, both needing a moment.

He picks up his cast off boxers. "Here, let me clean you up a little."

"I'll pop to the bathroom." I tell him.

"Oh, we're nowhere near finished yet, Sooks. Just give me a minute and then we're going to do this all over again."

And we do. All night long, on every available surface with the exception of Belle's room. Finally, in the early hours, we curl up together in his bed, and he pulls me into his arms and kisses the top of my head.

"I'm glad you trust me, Scott." I tell him. "I would never try to trap you."

"I know you wouldn't." He murmurs into my ear. "But the biggest difference is that if you got pregnant, I realised I wouldn't think it was the end of the world. Now go to sleep, or I'm going to want to have my way with you again."

I think about what he just said. This man who used to infuriate me beyond measure, now holds my heart in his hands. And it just feels so right.

———

THE NEXT MORNING, Scott gets Belle ready and into her bouncer and he brings me coffee and toast in bed. I hutch up against the pillows and smile, rubbing at my eyes.

"Figured you'd be thirsty and have worked up an appetite."

"I have. But I'm not sure my appetite is for toast."

"Deacon's coming." He says and it's like he's just soaked my libido in icy-cold water.

"When?"

"This afternoon."

"Do you need me to call Jenson to change my shift?"

"No. I can deal with Deacon and I'd rather it was just the two of us. I can't know whether or not it's going to be pleasant, so let's enjoy the rest of the morning, go out for lunch with Belle near InHale and then we'll walk with you to work before we come back here."

"Did you mean what you said about my moving in here?" I blurt out, having had the thoughts in my head. I've never been in any kind of serious relationship to know how to handle it. I just need to know where I stand, or whether his words came from a place of panic.

"Yes." He sits next to me on the bed. "I want you here every single night. You belong here in this bed."

"But it's all so fast."

"So should I give Belle back then, because she happened fast too. Well, in terms of her just being handed to me. I've known you longer. If she's staying, why can't you?"

I smile. "Please tell me she is staying. That Morgan isn't going to get her back."

"Morgan won't touch our daughter again."

Our daughter. My heart leaps in my chest.

"Two females came into my home recently, and two females are staying." He kisses me tenderly. "Now get your breakfast, get dressed, and let's get to the park."

———

AS I PUSH Belle in her pushchair, Scott at my side with his arm around me, I think about how pretty damn near perfect this is. I cannot know, but I hope this is our future, the three of us together, a family; two people Belle can rely on to meet her every need. I'm sure there are going to be hard times ahead. Scott and I have to get to know each other better and raise a kid at the same time, but as I take a deep breath of the fresh air around me, I'm prepared to take a chance this time; to let my defences down and embrace the possibilities.

I can't wait to see Carl's face when I tell him who the love of my life is and that I'm moving in...

CHAPTER TWENTY-THREE

Scott

Trepidation fills me as I slide the key into the lock knowing that Deacon's going to visit. He's never been here and I'm sure my little flat will be beneath him. I'm actually surprised he didn't demand that I meet him somewhere more... pretentious.

Leaving Belle to sleep, I have a quick tidy up. I tell myself that I don't care what he thinks of my home, but I think I'm lying. He lives a life of wealth and luxury and here I am in my run of the mill, two-bed London flat.

Anger stirs within me that the only reason he has everything he does is because he had the means. He had the best education he could get while I was stuck in our local comprehensive and while I was caring for my mum in her last days, he was living it up at university and making preparations to take the publishing world by storm.

I remember the way Dad's eyes used to light up whenever he spoke about Deacon like he was the best thing since sliced bread.

I'm still washing up when the buzzer rings out. Sucking in a calming breath, I dry my hands and walk over to allow him into the building. The temptation to leave him standing down there like an idiot does enter my mind but I don't need to sit here wondering what he's planning. Better to just get it all over with.

I open the front door and wait for his footsteps to fill my ears as he climbs the stairs. I try to look bored already when him and his fancy suit fill the space in front of me.

"No lift?" He raises a brow looking offended that I made him climb the stairs.

"No, no butler either," I quip, regretfully inviting him inside.

The flat feels smaller the second he steps in and it feels like he sucks all the air right out of it. He makes a show of looking around. His eyes zeroing on the washing up I was doing.

"What do you want, Deacon? What's so important that you had to visit?"

"I wanted to meet my niece. Where is she?"

Any normal person would have already seen her sitting in her bouncer by the sofa, but Deacon is no normal person.

I roll my eyes at him and turn away. "Would you like a drink?"

"No."

"Okay, well, Belle is right there." I point her out, feeling ridiculous for having to do so and not once removing my eyes from him.

"Hmmm..." he stares at my daughter who looks back at him with intrigue filling her eyes, either that or she's having a shit. "Really yours, huh?"

"Yes. Why, would you like to claim she's actually yours and take something else from me?"

He turns my way, his eyes assessing, but he says nothing, just judges.

I try again. "What do you want, Deacon?"

"Here." Reaching into his pocket, he pulls out an envelope and passes it over.

"What the hell is this?"

"Open it and you'll probably find out."

Hoping it'll make him leave faster, I rip it open and pull out the contents. "What the fuck is this?" I stare down at the cheque in my hand.

"Probably nowhere near what you're owed."

"Owed? I'm pretty sure I'm not owed anything."

"Really? Because every time you look at me all I see is jealousy. Take that, buy a new place to live that either has a lift, or even better, a front door on the ground floor. Make a life for your daughter that you can be proud of, give her everything you didn't have."

"I don't want your money," I spit, throwing the slip of paper back towards him. It doesn't get anywhere near him and just floats to the floor.

"Don't see it as my money, see it as Dad's. Take what you always deserved because I have every intention of ensuring he gets what he does."

"What the hell is that supposed to mean?"

"Nothing you need to know. Just take it and make a life for your daughter and that feisty woman you've got yourself."

My hackles rise. "Don't talk about Suki like that." A slow smirk curls at his lips.

"Shame, I bet she's a fucking riot in the sack." My fists clench, my chest swelling with hatred for this man who's meant to be my brother.

"Get out."

"With pleasure, *brother*."

He steps towards the door, surprisingly looking fondly at Belle.

"Before I go, you don't need to worry about the mother any longer. She won't be bothering you again."

"What did you do?"

"Let's just say she had a party for one with her favourite poison." He turns his back like it's the kind of thing he says on a daily basis.

"What the fuck does that mean?"

"She's gone, Scott." And with that he vanishes down the stairs.

I shut the door and fall back against it. *"She's gone, Scott."* Does that mean what I think it does?

Not wanting to put too much thought into what Deacon may or may not have done to get rid of my problem, I push from the door and head towards Belle. A piece of paper catches my eye before I get there and bending down to pick it up, I hold it in front of me.

That one piece of paper holds more money

than I've ever known in my life. I don't want his pity money, just staring at it makes me feel sick, but then Belle makes a gurgling noise and I look up to her.

"This is yours, baby girl. Daddy's going to make sure you get everything you could ever want."

THE FIRST THING Suki does when she gets home after her shift is ask how things went with Deacon. I'm not surprised by the question. She was adamant that she wanted to be here to support me, but she'd already spent enough time with him as far as I was concerned; she was better off out of it.

"He said it's sorted. He didn't really give me any details, but I think it's safe to assume we won't be seeing her again... ever." Suki pales slightly. "Too late to look guilty, Sooks. You dance with the devil and this is what happens."

"I'm not feeling guilty. She deserved everything she had coming at her. I just wish for Belle's sake that she had a decent mother."

"She has, Sooks. She's got the best mother in the whole world." Walking over to her, I press my front to her back and wrap my arms around her waist. She sighs and instantly relaxes against my touch. "He gave me money."

"What?" she asks, spinning in my arms.

"He gave me *a lot* of money. Said it was what I deserved and that I should use it to get a better place to live."

She tenses once again, her lips pressing into a thin line. "He did what? How fucking dare he? He—"

"Shush. It's okay." I stroke my thumb down her cheek and she relaxes. "He's right. This place isn't really ideal. It's too small for the three of us, there's no outside space for Belle, and the stairs are a fucking ball ache. I do think we should start looking for somewhere new, somewhere for the three of us, but—"

"But?"

"I don't want to use his money. Actually, we can't use his money."

"Why, what have you done?"

"I've already opened an account in Belle's name and deposited the cheque into it. No one can touch it until she's eighteen."

"Wow, okay. Um... how much was it?"

I lean forward and whisper the figure in her ear.

She pulls back, her eyes as wide as saucers. "Fucking hell, Scott. That's one rich baby you've got there."

"I told you he was loaded."

"I know but... shit. He wanted you to have that?"

"Fuck knows what he was thinking. No one ever knows what Deacon's thinking. It's probably blood money he needed off his hands or something."

"And you gave it to your daughter?"

"It'll just be money to her in eighteen years. Just think of the university she could go to, the travelling she could do, the house she could buy."

A smile twitches at her lips. "I think it's perfect, Scott. Nothing less than she deserves. And I also agree about this place. Let's sit down, work out our finances with your new hours and we'll see what we can come up with. I'll let my lease go and we can start searching."

"We're planning a life together, Sooks. Can you believe it?"

She laughs. "No, I really, really can't; but

equally, I can't think of anything I want to do more than spend my life making yours hell."

"Pain in the arse," I mutter before finding her lips and beginning the rest of our lives right here in the middle of the kitchen.

EPILOGUE

Scott

Six Months later

It took us four months to find our perfect family home. It was a little out of our price range but we both made a few sacrifices and eagerly signed on the dotted line. I could have made it easy for us by keeping Deacon's money, but I've never done things the easy way. I also didn't want to embark on our new life as a family knowing that we relied on him. I don't rely on my family. A lesson I learnt years ago. The only people I rely on are the ones under this roof.

"Scott, you need to get the fuck out of here," Sarah shouts through the door.

"Who the hell instructed you to be in charge?" I bark back but she knows I'm joking... I hope.

"Your darling soon-to-be wife. Now get a fucking move on. You're not even wearing a suit. What could possibly be taking you so long?"

"All right, all right, I'm going."

The night we moved in here, surrounded by boxes, I dropped to one knee and asked Suki to make it official. I know when she told Morgan that she was my fiancée that it was out of desperation, but from that day forward I saw her as mine. I just needed to bide my time, to do it the right way... the way she deserved. So with a simple princess-cut engagement ring, I asked her to do me the honour of insulting and abusing me for the rest of my life. With a laugh and tears streaming down her face she dropped to her knees with me and said yes. Aside from the day Belle appeared, it was the best fucking day of my life.

I was finally complete. I had my feisty little

woman and my incredible daughter. Things couldn't get any better.

I pull the door to the spare room open and find Sarah on the other side with her hands on her hips. She's dressed as Suki demanded in a pair of jeans and a blouse and her hair and make-up has been expertly done.

"You look beautiful."

"Getting second thoughts? Thinking you shouldn't have passed me up?" she asks with a laugh.

"Nah, you actually like me." She rolls her eyes, but loops her arm through mine and escorts me to my own front door. "I do know the way, you know."

"There's a car waiting at the curb for you. Make sure you go straight there."

"Where the fuck else would I go?"

"I don't know. You can be unpredictable."

"I'll be there, just make sure she is." Sarah nods and shuts the door in my face. *Nice.*

The car she mentioned is actually her husband's and he sits in the driver's seat waiting for me. "She really doesn't trust me to get there does she?"

He laughs but puts his foot down the second

I'm inside. "She just thought you deserved better than an Uber on your wedding day."

My wedding day. The words send chills up my spine. For years I said never. Never to marriage, never to kids, never to the same woman twice. But then with the arrival of one little unexpected package everything changed. And changed for the better. I can't imagine my life now without the two of them by my side.

Only minutes later, Emmett is pulling into the car park behind the registry office where we decided to say our vows and we're getting out and heading inside.

I greet the staff and they quickly get me into place with Emmett at my side. Both him and Sarah have been incredibly supportive over the last few months and I couldn't picture anyone else standing next to me for this.

"Are you ready? She's here?"

The lady doesn't wait for an answer. Instead, she turns to leave and the music filling the room changes.

"Last chance to run," Emmett warns.

"I'm good." I rub my trembling palms down the front of my trousers and straighten my shirt. Suki point blank refused to allow me to wear a suit. She insisted that she didn't want all the frills and fuss that comes with a wedding and that if we were doing this, then we were doing it our way. So after a very simple ceremony here, we're heading to InHale where we've got the private function room for the evening to celebrate with our closest friends and family. And that will include Deacon, who turns up once a week to visit his niece and acts almost human when he does so. Though I'll never completely trust him, so far, for six whole months he's just spoiled my daughter and then left us in peace. We even talk to each other and I'm slowly realising that my father wasn't much of one to him either. Looks like Giles Sullivan liked to play us off against each other for his own amusement.

The doors open and a few people rush inside including Jenson and Leah, and my auntie who's already got a tissue in her hand. Rolling my eyes at her, I focus my attention to the doors once again. No one is more surprised than me when my brother slips through the door, taking a seat at the back. I didn't bloody invite him, but as his eyes meet mine, we nod at each other.

Sarah appears, dressed as she was earlier, and walks down towards me. Then the music changes once again and my breath catches when she appears.

She told me that she was point blank not wearing white. I told her I didn't give a fuck what she wore as long as I got to put a ring on her finger, but as she takes her first step, I realise that she was right. White would have been wrong; it's not her. The short, red lace dress she's wearing however is so Suki. It's cut low at the front, giving me a great view of her incredible tits and flares out at the waist until the fabric sits just above her knees. Beside her is Carl, also dressed in his jeans, and in her arms is our baby girl, and she's the one wearing white.

My breath catches at the sight of my girls walking towards me. My world.

Her walk towards me seems to take forever, but at the same time it seems only seconds later that she hands Belle to Sarah and turns to me.

I forget about the people around us. I forget where we are. I forget that she's wearing bright-red lipstick and I pull her to me and kiss her like it could be our last. Cheers sound out around us and when I pull back, the registrar is looking at us with an amused smirk, but I don't give a shit because Suki and I have never done things by the book. We do things our way because it's the only way that works.

Turning back to my girl, I take in her smeared lips and the love that pours from her eyes as she stares back at me.

"I love you, Sooks."

"I love you too. Shall we do this then?"

"Fuck yes. Let's make you mine."

THE END

This is the last in the series of Hot Daddies, but prepare for the dark, dangerous, and glitzy world of B.A.D. Inc.

Meet Deacon King in **Torment**.

ALSO BY ANGEL & TRACY

HOT SINGLE DAD ROMANCE

#1 HOT DADDY SAUCE

#2 BABY DADDY RESCUE

#3 THE DADDY DILEMMA

#4 SINGLE DADDY SEDUCTION

#5 HOT DADDY PACKAGE

BAD INC BILLIONAIRES

#1 TORMENT

#2 RIDE

#3 BAIT

#4 PROVOKE

#5 BREAK

ABOUT ANGEL DEVLIN

Angel Devlin writes stories as hot as her coffee. She lives in Sheffield with her partner, son, and a gorgeous whippet called Bella.

Newsletter:
Sign up here for Angel's latest news and exclusive content.
https://geni.us/angeldevlinnewsletter

ABOUT TRACY LORRAINE

Tracy Lorraine is new adult and contemporary romance author. Tracy is in her thirties and lives in a cute Cotswold village in England with her husband and daughter. Having always been a bookaholic with her head stuck in her Kindle, Tracy decided to try her hand at a story idea she dreamt up and hasn't looked back since.

Be the first to find out about new releases and offers. Sign up to my newsletter here.

If you want to know what I'm up to and see teasers and snippets of what I'm working on, then you need to be in my Facebook group. Join Tracy's Angels here.

Keep up to date with Tracy's books at
www.tracylorraine.com

Printed in Great Britain
by Amazon